LITTLE

TRENTON SECURITY BOOK 2

J.M. DABNEY

HOSTILE WHISPERS PRESS, LLC

REMEMBER:

This book is a work of fiction. All characters, places, and events are from the author's imagination and should not be confused with fact. Any resemblance to persons, living or dead, events or places, is purely coincidental.

PLEASE BE ADVISED:

This book contains material that is only suitable for mature readers. It may contain scenes of a sexual nature and violence.

AUTHOR'S NOTE

This story contains scenes of extreme depictions of childhood trauma/violence. While it's not written in great detail some readers may find the content objectionable.

To my Readers

CONTENTS

PROLOGUE

COLLINS, MISSISSIPPI 2001

*H*armon Little hung his head as he stared down at the stained sheet he'd dragged across his lap. He smelled of stale beer, cigarette smoke, and sex. He hid his face to conceal the tears as the woman on the opposite side of the bed got dressed. She'd screamed when she'd awakened to find him watching her sleep. He'd started to brush her soft blonde hair from her face.

He'd just wanted to touch her. He liked touching—it made him feel like he was real. Not just a thing. Disposable and broken, that's what he felt like after all the men and women used him. At fifteen, he didn't know anything but the life he had lived since he'd run away. He didn't much care for the sex. He always regretted it afterward, but the touching was nice. He'd suffer just to feel loved even if it was a lie.

The girl had wanted him last night. She'd held him close and said his name. Whispered it like he was special, but now she looked at him as if he were disgusting.

Choking back a sob, he turned his body away and attempted to hide behind the sheet he pulled up to his chest.

"Are you fucking crying? What kinda man cries like a baby?"

He flinched and tried to make himself smaller—invisible. Even as the tears quickly slipped down his cheeks, he watched her from the corner of his eye. He wanted to pull the memories of the night closer to shield himself from the disdain.

"A boy with a dick your size, shame you can't use it. Such a fucking waste." She spat the vile words in his direction as she hopped around while she was slipping her shoes on.

He jerked his gaze to the front and stared at the peeling paint and crumbling wall. He didn't look at her as he listened to the click of her heels when she left his dirty room in an abandoned warehouse. He had a filthy mattress on the floor that he'd covered in trash bags. His clothes were shoved into a duffel. He'd have to scrounge change later to hit the laundry mat.

He'd considered that place home for almost two years since his last foster family called social services to come get him. He'd run before they had arrived. He didn't mean to wear out his welcome. All he wanted was someone of his own—a family who wouldn't throw him away.

He remembered a mom. She had hair his favorite color—yellow. Or at least he thought it was yellow. He'd sat on the floor of the social service's waiting room drawing a picture.

The nice lady had asked his mom was she sure, he hadn't understood until his mom had said that she hated him and didn't want to be his mommy anymore.

The lady held him as he cried and tried to call her back, but she hadn't even slowed down. Her heels had tapped a lot like the woman who'd just left.

He just wanted to be loved.

The men were worse because they just bent him over and fucked him. When they were done, they'd pushed him to the ground. They'd do up their pants and walk away after throwing money at him. At least the women let him have a night on occasion. He'd have to wait until they were asleep and he'd ease across the bed, slow as not to wake them up. He'd press his forehead against their arm, if he was lucky they smelled sweet and their skin would be soft. But again, it usually ended the same, a wad of money on the nightstand and forgotten as quickly as he was out of sight.

The woman who'd just left him, he'd thought she liked him. She'd smiled at him. Touched him and had even pressed her lips to his. He loved the kisses so much. He didn't get those very often. He couldn't remember the time before last night.

The tears started to fall again, and he angrily swiped at his cheeks. He shoved his bare feet into his unlaced boots and pushed the sheet aside. He surged to his feet and stomped over to his pack he'd hidden in the wall. He moved a piece of sheetrock to the side and pulled out his bag, and then he dug out a clean, threadbare towel and his only set of clean clothes.

There was a spigot where he could clean up, the water was cold, but he couldn't show his face at the shelter anymore this week. Suspicion grew every time, and he couldn't afford for them to call the cops or social services. His life was hell. Yet he didn't want to go back only to be rejected again.

An old friend of his got himself an apartment. Sometimes they'd allow him to come by and take a shower. A real one where he didn't have to be on a time limit. He had gone a few weeks ago, so he didn't want to wear out his welcome.

He strode naked through the warehouse. The steps creaked and swayed a bit under his feet. He darted through the break in the wall and ran for the little enclosure he'd made. He hung his clothes on a few metal hangers he'd found, then pulled the mat down he'd cleaned and dried from hooks after his last shower. The broken hose he'd salvaged from the dump worked well enough with the old rusty bucket.

If nothing else he survived okay, but he wanted to do better than okay. He had a sliver of soap remaining, and he'd used it to wash the stench and memories away. He didn't look at himself or let his touch linger; he didn't want to know what they thought was so disgusting about him.

He knew he wasn't pretty. He was too big and hairy for his age, but he thought he was nice. Maybe he wasn't right in the head sometimes, but—he lowered his head as the tears started again. He reached for the rusty razor, drew it lightly across his wrist and wished he could do it this time.

He just wanted to know, why couldn't someone just love him?

DO YOU LOVE ME?

PRESENT DAY

The moon hung brightly in the sky, an owl hooted in the distance, and Harmon stared up from where he was lying with his head on his best friend's thigh. Lily was old enough to be his mother, but she was probably the best friend he'd ever had. There was no judgment of his crazy antics. He didn't have to pretend to be something he wasn't.

Her fingers rubbed circles on the top of his head as he passed her the blunt. He'd never had parents, and he only faintly remembered a mother. Her hair was blonde, and she had bright green eyes to match his, but he didn't know if he'd conjured what he assumed his mother looked like. The memories faded more each year, and he didn't fight it. He had no memory of a father at all; maybe the rest should fade as easily.

Lily stared off into space as she smoked. When he'd met her son Lucky years before, and then her, he'd been jealous. She was what he'd dreamed a mother would be. Honest, loving, and slightly insane like him. Everyone had given him shit for being too out there. It wasn't like he'd meant to be, he just couldn't help it. Sometimes the shit that came out of his mouth shocked even him.

"Do you love me," he asked and was instantly embarrassed that he had.

She smacked his forehead and then went back to caressing his scalp with her nails. "Stupid question, of course, I love you, you're perfect."

He smiled at the serene expression on her face. He took the still smoking blunt back, placed it between his lips and inhaled deeply.

"But you're not fucking my husband."

He choked, and his lungs burned, and all Lily did was laugh as she looked down at him.

"What the fuck, Lily, he's like my dad. Hot Dad, but still Dad."

"Pervert. So, why the question? Don't I make it clear enough?"

"I went on a date the other night."

To be honest, he hadn't wanted to go on the date. He'd fucked up several months previous and slept with someone he shouldn't have. His dick and insecurity had gotten his best friend's boyfriend kidnapped. He had just wanted to touch someone, and the man had let him kiss him. He wasn't proud that he would've sold his soul for that kiss. All of that had blinded him as to what was really going down during that bathroom fuck session.

The guy hadn't looked at him while he fucked him, but the before had been nice. The guy had just bent over for him, and he should've noticed the man's fake groans and dirty talk. At the time, it hadn't mattered so much as someone seemed to want him.

"Oh, please tell me you have details, hot, sweaty, nasty, can't walk right details."

And that was one of the reasons he loved Lily. She didn't let life get her down. That could have something to do with the copious amounts of weed the woman smoked on the daily. But it didn't change how he envied her *don't give a fuck* attitude.

"No, he skipped out, said he had to go to the bathroom."

The number of times he'd had dates skip out on him would be comical if it weren't so fucking sad.

"Then he wasn't worth your time. As I've said, you're perfect, Harmon. Just like my own biological spawn."

"Would you adopt me?"

"Already did. The moment you stepped into my house you were mine, just like with Priest, and Hunter and Wren. You're just as special as Linus, Lou, and Lucky, and all my sons-in-law."

"Do you think I'm unlovable?"

"Of course not, do you think I am?"

"No," he shouted and then grimaced.

"Harmon, my sweet, crazy son." She stroked his jaw.

He almost felt like crying. It wasn't the first time she'd called him son and even Lily's husband, Damon did it sometimes. Damon made sure to kiss the top of his head like he did with their children and their partners. He was never left out. It was odd, and the first few times he'd mentally questioned their intentions; what they wanted from him.

"One of these days you'll meet someone just like I met Damon. It won't be perfect. Others might not get it. But they don't have to."

"How will I know?"

He'd dreamed of having a relationship like Lily and Damon's. Love and acceptance without conditions, it was almost too perfect, but like Lily had mentioned, people might not get it.

"Oh, if you're like me and since you're my kid, it'll hit you. You'll look at someone someday, and it'll be like lightning struck. It'll be primal. And perfect. I went home with Damon the first night I met him. We've barely been apart since."

"Isn't that a little quick?"

"When it's right, it's right. Don't tell me you haven't bedded someone the first night you met them."

"Fuck no, but that was fucking, nothing emotional." He didn't want to talk about all the men and women who'd paid to fuck him in his past. It embarrassed him. He wasn't ashamed he survived just how he'd gone about it. He'd had sex maybe a handful of times since he turned eighteen promising himself that the next would be special. Unfortunately, that hadn't happened.

"You'll find him, Harmon, or her."

"They'll think I'm too crazy."

Lilly gave him another slap, and he rubbed his forehead.

"There's nothing crazy about you. You're unique, and the world is filled enough with carbon copies of the same. Be you, and your person will come along when you need them to."

His other mother-figure, Peaches, and Lily apparently learned how to be a mother from the same handbook. That was exactly something Peaches had said to his friend Livingston when Liv had doubts about the man he wanted.

"Are you two coming in for dinner or not," Damon yelled from the back door.

He laughed as Lily held up the relit blunt and listened to Damon's heavy sigh. The older man appeared and took it, but not before he placed a kiss on Lily's upturned lips. It might sound weird to others, but Lily and Damon were the perfect couple. Damon doted on his eccentric wife. He'd caught little things over the time he'd been around.

Damon fed Lily before he even made himself a plate. He touched her constantly when they were close. It was envy-inducing. But Lily said meeting your person was like being struck by lightning—he wondered if that were true.

"Okay, you two, dinner, now."

He rolled to his feet, and the world spun a bit, he let out a laugh as he grabbed Lily's hands and hauled her to her feet. She wrapped her arms around him and hugged him tightly. He lifted his head from where he'd buried his face against her throat. Damon watched them seemingly content and happy, and he wondered if he'd ever meet someone who made him that happy simply by being.

He let Lily drag him into the house. Lily's plate was already full and sitting in front of her usual spot. He released her hand and went to grab the empty plate.

"Son, I already made your plate, sit."

Damon pointed toward the table and nudged him. He'd assumed the plate was for Damon.

"Oh, thanks." Damon did that for his kids. The kids plates were always made first, then Lily's. He sat down and stared at the plate overflowing with food. A grown man shouldn't tear up, but Damon hugged him and kissed the top of his head.

Damon poured himself and Lily wine, then Little covered his glass before a bottle of apple juice was placed beside his wineglass.

"Like I wouldn't know what my kids like," Damon muttered and settled in.

They ate and talked. It was just like all those silly dreams from when he was a kid. It was hard to accept, and he pretended it didn't affect him. Luckily, Lily and Damon didn't call him on it. He tried to relax and just enjoy before he had to head home. His place wasn't nice but it was a roof, and that's all he cared about.

* * *

SAFETY WAS ONLY a fond dream as he darted through the crowds. Linus was going to kick his ass for this one. He'd crashed at Lily and Damon's when he should've been home. Those two were way too loud, and he was too stoned to drive, so he'd left straight from their house to work. No sleep and still buzzed. It would've figured someone would spot his big ass.

A week of tracking down some wanna-be gangster who was trying to unload a small quantity of uncut diamonds. The dude who owned the local jewelry store had a history of taking in stolen goods, but not since the man moved to Powers. It seemed he wanted to get back to his illegal activities and all the perks which came with that.

He glanced over his shoulder just as two mean looking security guys turned the corner, and he started into the store. Hoping like hell they hadn't seen him.

"Little, quit running," Brody, one of the cashiers, yelled at him. Brody was married to a friend of his named Trouble.

He waved as he pivoted and headed down an aisle. One minute he was hitting top stride, and then he smashed into something and looked down to find a tiny man sprawled across the floor.

"Oh shit, man, are you okay?" He fell to his knee beside the stranger. He checked for damage. He was a good fifty pounds heavier than the man he'd just taken out.

"I'm...I'm fine."

The man's voice was soft and sweet. Oh, he liked the sound of that. He straightened the man's cute black framed glasses on his even cuter pug nose. His face was kind of narrow and his eyes rounded, the brightest fucking blue he'd ever seen. Then it was like five rapid punches to the gut.

Was this what Lily—he widened his eyes.

Boots pounding and Brody yelling for more people to stop running, he knew he was seconds from apprehension, but he wasn't leaving the little man behind. Would he see him again if he did?

"Come with me," he ordered and grabbed the protesting man's arm and hauled him toward the rear exit. The owner of the store just waved as he passed.

Yeah, everyone knew he wasn't right, and it worked to his advantage.

He circled back around to his van, the man wasn't protesting, but that might be the shock he could see in the stranger's pretty eyes. Whatever worked, as long as it lasted until he got the stranger home.

He shoved the man into the vehicle and climbed over him to get to the driver's seat. He calmly did a U-turn and pulled out, headed for the highway and home.

WAS HE JUST KIDNAPPED?

The scenery flew by in a blur, Solomon Poe tried to remember the classes he took on self-defense. Did you open the door and tuck and roll? They said never let them take you to the second location. Oh my goodness, he was going to die. Either by breaking his neck when he threw himself from a moving vehicle or when the smiling man beside him got to wherever the stranger was taking him. He reached for the door handle and heard the lock click.

"Don't think about it."

That wasn't creepy at all.

One minute he'd been looking at diet pills and protein bars, and the next he was trapped inside some strange man's van. What if he pretended to faint or something? Would the guy pull the vehicle over to give him a chance to run? Then he groaned at the running part because he would hyperventilate after a few feet.

He jiggled his belly and sighed. He was going to die.

The van veered suddenly, and he almost fell between the seats. He braced his hands-on the hardest thigh he'd ever felt in his life. There was more muscle in that one leg than he had in his entire body. They pulled up to a warehouse. The metal exterior was rusted, and the windows shuttered. The man reached up and hit what looked like a garage door opener. Two massive doors creaked open, and then they drove slowly inside.

The interior was pitch black, and his eyes squinted as flood-lights came on. He unlocked the door and clawed at the handle, he was out of the van within seconds and ran for the slowly closing doors. He knew once they locked he was trapped.

He mentally yelled *yes* as he slipped through the doors and instantly stopped in his tracks. He turned to find his shirt trapped in the closed doors. He ripped his bow tie loose and was just working loose the buttons on his bright yellow shirt when a shadow crossed over him.

"What do you think you're doing?"

What did he think he was doing? What kind of stupid—

He sighed as he looked down at himself. His paisley bow tie lay dusty and rumpled on the ground, and his shirt opened to expose his pale, hairless chest. This was how he was going to die.

The guy seemed so calm and collected. Of course he was, the man was going to kill him and hide his body, and no one would look for him. No one who'd worry until the smell of his decom-posing body alerted them to his presence.

"You're not answering me."

The big guy blinked his eyes, the thick fringe of his lashes caressed his broad cheekbones. The man looked almost innocent, well as innocent as a suspected sociopathic serial killer could.

"I'm trying or was trying to escape."

"Oh. I did this shit all wrong."

The guy dug a phone out of his back pocket and seemed to hit speed dial. Was he calling his partner? Oh shit, he was going to be killed by two crazy people now.

"Lily, I think I did something wrong."

The sweet feminine voice coming over the speaker reassured him for a minute until what she said registered.

"When all else fails, a shovel and lye, son."

"No, lightning struck, or more like five rapid to the gut. Made me feel like I needed to puke."

Wasn't that...attractive?

"Oh, oh, I'm so happy, who's your person? It's not a cop, is it? I can only handle one cop son-in-law."

Person? Son-in-law? What was going on?

"Um, I may have kidnapped him without realizing it?"

May have kidnapped? This was a kidnapping, buddy.

"Kidnapping, that's so romantic!"

Romantic, romantic, was the woman, hell, this appeared to be the crazy man's mother.

"Who did our son kidnap?"

There was another one, but this voice was calmer and whiskey smooth and sounded a bit bored.

"Lightning struck, made him feel like he wanted to puke."

"Congratulations, son, bring your person for Sunday dinner to meet everyone."

Were these people not understanding the concept of kidnapping?

"I don't think he likes me very much."

Oh no, he would not feel remorse by being assaulted by huge, sad eyes that may appear slightly watery.

"Of course he does, Harmon, he just needs to get to know you. You didn't take him home, did you? Your place was a fucking disaster when I brought you your trees the other day."

"I cleaned, Lily."

"I don't see why you don't let me hire you a cleaning person... they have some great nude options. I could get you a man and woman team."

"I don't need strangers in my place. I gotta talk to him, I'll call you—"

"Call if you need bail money, we set you up a fund. We love you, Harmon."

"Love y'all too, bye." The man disconnected the call and raised his hand to rub the back of his neck and worried the ring through his bottom lip. "You're gonna make me beg and apologize, ain't ya?"

As soon as Harmon finished the question, the doors started to open, and he almost fell, but strong hands steadied him, then the man stepped back.

"You kidnapped me." He momentarily felt stupid for stating the obvious, but he had to admit he was frazzled.

"I wasn't thinking."

"Apparently." He was feeling bitchy, and his super cute kidnapper pouting made him feel guilty for it.

"I'm sorry," Harmon mumbled.

"What was that?"

"I'm sorry, okay, there I said it."

"You know apologies work better when you actually sound remorseful."

"I'm not."

"Of course you're not."

"I'm Harmon Little, but everyone just calls me Little."

There wasn't anything little about the man in front of him. The man was so big that it cast him in shadow. Introductions should make him worried, didn't that mean imminent death because he knew the man's name and description?

"Solomon Poe."

A broad smile pulled at the corners of Harmon's wide mouth. "Pretty name. You're wearing my favorite color."

The man seemed to reach for him before he clenched his fists and shoved his hands behind his back.

"Can you take me back to my car now?"

Little hesitated long enough for him to start worrying.

"I might have to call someone else to take you."

"Why?"

"I fucked up a job. I got made, and they'll be looking for me."

"Will they—"

"No, they didn't see you, but they definitely…Linus is going to

16

be so pissed. They'll put my baby on the roof again. Do you know how much of a bitch it is to get a van off a roof? Fucking nightmare and that's after I can find it."

He'd wonder if he was drugged, maybe he was hallucinating from hunger. There was no appropriate food in his fridge, so he hadn't eaten breakfast. Maybe it's dehydration? His personal trainer pushed him every evening until his muscles screamed in pain. The guy was probably in the running for Sadist of the Year. He'd gotten home from working out and had fallen into bed hungry and exhausted. He was tired of being the pudgy guy no man wanted. He had six months before his thirtieth birthday, and he was going to be rocking six-pack abs if it killed him—it was going to kill him.

At the thought he realized his shirt was unbuttoned, he started to pick up his tie, but Harmon got to it first. He was uncomfortable with the way Harmon just watched him. He felt like a science project. The man rubbed the silky fabric of his tie between his thick, blunt fingers. He observed the way Harmon licked his lips, and he backed up into the pitch-black warehouse.

Opposite way, idiot, he scolded.

"I'll call you a ride." Harmon's words rushed past his lips, and he charged around him.

He was dizzy, one minute the man snatched him from a grocery store aisle, trapped him in a warehouse, and suddenly seemed like he couldn't get away fast enough. He pivoted on his toes and jogged to keep up. Once again spotlights came on and extinguished with their progression. He wondered if the man was scared of the dark or just paranoid, he would bet his last dollar it was paranoia.

A workspace with at least ten monitors and two overflowing trash cans of energy drinks set off to the side, and he approached as he kept an eye on Harmon's broad back. Harmon spun a large, worn desk chair and motioned for him to sit.

"Your mother seems…interesting."

"Not my mother, best friend."

Harmon punched a button on a landline phone and stood back with his arms crossed over his chest. His tie was crushed in Harmon's hand, but he thought better of asking for it back.

Best friend? She seemed more dementedly maternal than friend-like, but he didn't argue.

"Your fucking ass is in trouble." A gravelly and exceptionally scary voice filled the space.

"Don't start, dude, it wasn't my—"

"Little, it's never your fault...the boss was called away from his men."

"Shit."

A masculine yet soft giggle sounded, broken by an obscene moan. *Oh no, they couldn't be doing*—a high-pitched squeal sealed it. They were.

"Man, could you get your man off your dick for a minute while we talk."

"Not happening, my boy is staying right where he is."

There was a whispered, *I didn't tell you to stop, boy.*

This wasn't happening.

"I need you to transport a package for me."

"What about having my husband on my dick are you not getting?"

"Well, pound one out and do me this favor. You know you ain't happy if Fielding ain't limping."

"Give me an hour."

"Are you sure it won't be two?"

"I'll make sure he's good and ready—"

Harmon thankfully disconnected the call before the man could finish whatever statement he was about to make.

"Sorry about that, newlyweds, and," Harmon cleared his throat, "Liv's a bit...possessive."

"Okay."

"Would you like something to drink?"

"I guess, do you have more than…energy drinks?"

"Oh shit, I don't know." Harmon wrung his large hands, then grinned. "Apple juice!"

He was grabbed again, and the light show restarted, this time they walked into what looked to be the living area. No walls, no shadows, but this time Harmon turned on lamps beside a raggedy couch. Boxes upon boxes of snacks, bags of chips, there wasn't a non-processed food anywhere in the kitchen area.

Still holding his hand, Harmon opened the refrigerator, one whole shelf strained under the weight of cans of heart attack, along with the drawers at the bottom. The other shelf contained bottles of apple juice. Harmon didn't have food in there at all.

"I'm not going to run," he said as he tried to free his hand.

"Oh, sorry."

Harmon dropped his hand like it burned him.

He took the bottle of juice Harmon handed him.

"Can I have my tie back?"

"I don't know where it is."

His brows drew together as he watched Harmon shove the fabric deeper into his pocket. Harmon strode quickly to the couch and plopped down. He cringed at the crack of wood as it sounded like something broke.

"You can have my chair."

Harmon looked embarrassed and uncomfortable. He assumed this was a bachelor pad. He'd never been to another man's house before; he didn't even have male friends. To be honest, he didn't have friends at all. The closest he came to having one would be Grace. She owned a local thrift store, but they didn't hang out beyond the time it took him to shop.

He walked toward the recliner, turned and perched on the edge of the seat. The silence was thick, and Harmon sat there with his fingers linked, tapping his thumbs together. The man looked everywhere but at him. For someone who'd kidnapped him and wanted his company so much, Harmon was quiet and awkward.

"What is it you do for a living?"

"I work for a security company."

"Security guard?"

"No, electronic surveillance and sometimes bodyguard. Every so often one of my boss' husbands, Hunter, and me break security systems to test designs."

"Oh, sounds interesting. What does breaking security systems entail?"

"Some breaking and entering, Hunter deals with the computer part, and I'm more hands on. It's fun, and the money isn't bad."

Harmon's evident uneasiness at talking about himself caused his curiosity to intensify. The man was an enigma, in charge and then pulling back to the point of shutting down.

"What about the surveillance?"

"Planting bugs, cameras, following people, spending lots of time in my van taking pictures."

"Oh."

"I'm not a stalker!"

He jumped, and Harmon's mortification amused him. Harmon's eyes were wide and rounded. Okay, the big guy was kind of cute. This was the weirdest day of his life. He scooted farther back and relaxed into the thick cushions. He leaned his head on his raised palm to wait for the strange man to come pick him up.

The thought that he had to wait for a man to finish having sex with his husband to come pick him up caused him to shake his head. He sighed heavily and the adrenaline of the last hour rushed away, he yawned and fought sleep, but it pulled at him.

His head fell to the side, and his eyes popped open, the sight in front of him had him nearly swallowing his tongue. Dark brown skin shined with sweat, and loose work-out pants threatened to fall off slim hips. Massive fists wrapped in white tape brutally connected with a heavy bag. Bulky muscles shifted beneath smooth, tattooed skin. The man was absolutely physically perfect. Harmon shifted to expose rounded pecs with a spattering of black hair. His stomach wasn't cut, but he had that deep V that disappeared into the waistband of his shorts. He'd never been that close to those perfect indentions before.

He screamed as it sounded like someone was trying to take the door out.

"Liv, knock it the fuck off, he's sleeping, shit, was sleeping, asshole." Harmon hurried off mumbling curses.

He shot up from the chair and scrubbed his hands over his face, and then he attempted to smooth his wrinkled clothes. Checked to make sure he hadn't drooled. Harmon was approaching with a man that made even Harmon look small behind him. The first thing he noticed was the scars that covered almost all the exposed skin on the man's right side.

"This the package?"

"Yes, he just needs to go back to his car."

"And why is he here?"

"I might have borrowed him."

"Borrowed, is that code for retrieval missions, which ends with a life sentence for kidnapping?"

"Possibly."

The man groaned and scrubbed a broad hand over his face. "What are we going to do with you, Little?"

"I didn't mean to do it. Lily told me lightning strikes, and I grabbed him."

The new man loudly cursed and shook his head.

"What have we talked about when it comes to Lily? No advice when you two are high as fuck."

"We hadn't had that much to smoke."

"Whatever, I didn't know the package was a person. I brought my bike."

It was all too weird, the situation, people, he wanted to go home and forget this day happened. Something about that thought made him frown. As weird as Harmon was, the man was awkward and strangely sweet.

"He can have my helmet."

Harmon ran off and left him with the stranger.

"I'm Solomon."

"Livingston, everyone calls me Liv."

"Nice to meet you."

"You going to press charges?"

"What happens if I'm thinking about it?" He wasn't. Despite the kidnapping and weirdness, Harmon seemed harmless.

"You might not make it back to your vehicle."

"Liv, knock it off."

"I'm just saying."

"Here," Harmon said and handed him the helmet. "It might be a little big for you, but it should work to get you home. I'm...I'm sorry and if you—"

"It's fine. We'll just call it one of those surreal days and forget it ever happened, okay?"

The man deflated and dropped his chin, then turned his face away.

"Come on, my boy is at home waiting for me."

He didn't want any more details, so he rushed to catch up with Liv and walked out into the dying late afternoon light. He turned to look over his shoulder, but the doors creaked shut and blocked his view.

"If I were you, forget this day ever fucking happened. Leave Little alone. He ain't for you, little man."

He didn't know why that hurt, but it did, and he followed Liv's instructions on how to ride behind him. He gave the warehouse one more longing look and held on tight as Liv pulled off in a raining of gravel and dust.

WHEN WOULD HE LEARN
APPROPRIATE BEHAVIOR?

*I*nappropriate laughter threatened to escape, and he prepared to get fired. First, the unexpected kidnapping of a stranger. He still didn't know how the hell they were able to get his van on the roof, but they succeeded and he'd spent a fortune for the crane—again. He'd returned to the grocery store several times. Yet he hadn't spotted the bow tie wearing cutie. Getting with Poe was a lost cause, but that didn't help his disappointment. He decided on a distraction. The rest of the team didn't fall for his pranks. Raul and Pure were easy marks.

He'd spent all day attempting to lure the two men to the lower level of Trenton Security where they had the gun range and weapons lockers and cages. He didn't feel guilty about it either. Raul had focused his attention on Pure's ass. A quick shove from behind and he had both men locked up.

He raised his arm and wiggled his fingers at the two pissed off men. In his opinion, if they couldn't get their shit together they deserved it. They needed a bit of encouragement and he thought he was just the man to do that.

"Little, I'm tired of your shit, man."

As Raul's palm connected with the gate, the metal rattled.

Pure stared down the sniper scope of a rifle and he swore the man's trigger finger twitched.

"It's for your own good," he announced. "Now, I brought some educational tools along to help." He bent at the waist and dug the two anatomically correct puppets from his small gym bag. He hugged them both to his chest as he removed condoms and single-use lube from the bag, and then shoved the items through the cage.

"You gotta be fucking kidding me!" Raul threw himself against the door.

Did Raul think that was going to work?

"What the hell is going on?" Linus's voice boomed off the walls of the basement.

He struggled to get the puppets onto his hands and as his fingers worked the arms, he waved them in Linus's face. "Puppet show," he said.

Linus crossed his arms over his broad chest and rested back against the cage. "What happened last time you locked them up, Little?"

"Stitches. But scars heighten my bad boy exterior. It's sexy."

"And you think this time is going to end any different?"

"No, but it's puppets, man." He heard the hysterical glee in his voice.

"I think they get the idea of where to insert Tab A into Slot B."

"You're just going to fucking stand there?" Raul demanded. "I thought we agreed you'd keep his crazy ass away from me."

Raul had worked with them for years, but even being a newbie to the full-time team, the man should know better than to think he'd escape. He jerked his gaze to Linus to see if his boss was going to ruin his fun. Linus' smirk told him he wasn't going to help Little's victims. He mentally fist pumped at the nod that told him to proceed.

"You wearing your vest, Little?"

"Won't matter much with a head shot." Pure punctuated his

statement with the slow slide of the bolt as the man loaded the rifle.

"You're so violent, Pure, sexual frustration does that to a person. Now, this is mini-Raul." He held his puppet encased right hand. "And this cutie is mini-Pure."

"Just wait until I get out of this fucking cage. You're fucking dead."

"Now, now, Raul," he chided.

"Just let him do this, I'm interested to see what Little has to say. I got a pre-teen to have the sex talk with. You mind if I borrow those?"

"All yours, I got female ones too. They only sold them as a hetero set."

"Good deal."

"Let's begin with foreplay, kissing is important." He made smooching sounds as he pressed the puppet's faces together. "Oh, Raul..."

Pain shot through his ears at the reverberation as a single shot echoed in deafening decibels. "Fake Jesus, Pure, what the fuck?" He pushed the puppets to his ears as he bent at the waist.

"Pure, I don't care if you shoot Little, but, fuck, boy, that was too close," Linus yelled. "I'm gonna put you over my fucking knee."

"You touch me and I won't give you a warning shot," Pure growled.

He heard the ejection of one bullet casing as Pure loaded the second.

"I won't kill you, Little, but, you better open—"

"I was just trying to help, no need to be mean. Boss, you want to catch one?"

"Man, I need one."

He headed for the door with Linus beside him.

"What about us?" Raul asked.

"We'll let you out when Pure calms down."

"Try to be helpful, dude, and what the fuck do you get in return?"

"Ungrateful fuckers. We headed to Mama's place?"

"Yeah."

"Just wait until I get out of here. I'll kill both y'all's fucking asses. Linus, Little!" Raul cursed and banged against the cage behind them.

As he entered the elevator, he spun and had the puppets wave bye to the two pissed off men. Both their faces were red and then they turned on each other.

"You know, they gonna take your ass out, right?"

"It will be worth it. And I went through the trouble of special ordering these." He held up his hands. "And I get no thanks for it. Shameful, man."

"You do know you're on Cheating Spouse duty?"

"Yeah, yeah, I remember."

* * *

HE WAS STUCK on stakeout duty for the second week in a row. No action. No takedowns, just sitting in his van all night by himself. Plenty of time for him to think about his mistakes and he'd made plenty. It wasn't as if he meant to do it. He'd kidnapped someone just because he thought lightning struck. It would teach him to listen to Lily especially after two and a half blunts. The man hadn't even come looking for him and when Liv had returned his helmet, no note or anything.

Of course he didn't, Harmon, you kidnapped him. Little hated that voice of reason in his head.

"Little, you there," Pure's voice coming over his laptop scared the fuck out of him. He hadn't wanted to deal with an earpiece all night and had routed audio through his computer. Most nights he didn't hear anyone's voice other than his own.

Luckily, Pure forgave him. Even for being a bit reserved, Pure was laidback and had a decent sense of humor. It kind of helped that Pure got a shot in before him and Linus left Raul and Pure in the cage.

"Yeah, man, what's up?"

"You got a call. No name, just a number. You want it?"

"Sure." He memorized the number as Pure repeated the number twice.

Maybe it would be a distraction to kill some time until dawn, and he could go home to sleep. He was hoping his punishment would end soon. He didn't mind the surveillance shit, but it got boring after a while.

"They didn't leave a message?"

"No, just said to have you call him. Sounded kinda nervous."

He couldn't be that lucky, but he didn't want to take a chance. "Thanks, Pure." He barely waited for Pure to say goodbye before he was reaching for his phone and typing in the number.

*Please, please, let it be…*a sweet, shy hello made him smile. He'd remember that voice anywhere.

"Hello, Poe." Since he'd learned the man's name, he'd been Poe. It was cute and sweet, just like the man.

"Harmon, you called back."

"You didn't leave a name or message, just a number. I was hoping it was you."

"You were?"

"Fuck yeah, I was."

He needed to temper his excitement. The small, pretty man wearing his sexy bow ties wasn't for him.

"I'm not interrupting, am I? The gentleman I talked to said you were on an assignment."

"More on punishment than assignment."

"For kidnapping me?"

"No, screwing up a job, so I'm on cheating spouse duty. I spend a lot of time watching unfaithful people. I mess up a lot."

"Any in particular?"

"Oh yeah, dude's old lady is out of town for a business trip. Overseas for a month, in two weeks there's been three different women alternating nights. I saw his wife. She's gorgeous. All soft and pretty, these side pieces, no meat at all."

"Oh, you're—"

"Bi."

He knew that was a deal breaker for some people. He didn't question that he was attracted to people. He didn't care what was or wasn't in their pants. He didn't have any prerequisites for dating anyone, except he wanted someone who treated him like he mattered.

"That's why the lady on the phone said your person."

"Yeah. Why did you call?"

"I don't know, you left an impression."

"That's kinda putting it mildly. I've never kidnapped anyone before."

Poe's chuckle made him grin.

"I'm feeling special."

Poe's sweet voice went low and husky, was Poe flirting?

"You should, you were very pretty."

"And I was wearing your favorite color?"

"That too. Would you like to have dinner with me or we can just hang out with my friends, no pressure or anything."

"I'd like to have dinner."

"You want to come to my van?"

"Aren't you working?"

"I can't get in any more trouble. I'll have Lily deliver me leftovers. I'm sorry, that's not really romantic, I'm—"

"Don't apologize, I'm an insomniac, so I don't sleep all that much. Why don't I pick up dinner and bring it?"

"I don't have any cash on me."

"You get the next one."

"Okay."

"What would you like?"

"Surprise me. I'm not picky when it comes to food."

"Tell me where I should meet you."

He gave Poe the address and told him to meet him on the corner. Then he'd sneak him to the van. He might always be in trouble, but he didn't want to get yelled at in front of Poe. That would be embarrassing. He really wanted that next one Poe mentioned. A proper date where he picked Poe up at his place, and they went to a nice restaurant.

He disconnected the call and stalked his phone, checking the time and messages. Impatient for Poe to show up. His legs bounced, and he was nervous, maybe Poe liked him enough that he could have a goodnight kiss.

He felt stupid and tossed the offending device aside so he'd stop looking at it. He wasn't a street kid anymore. He didn't have to suffer through just for the scraps.

He watched the monitors as he waited. The guy still hadn't come out, but the man had been spending the night with the other women since his wife was out of town. Any other time he just did an hour or two, then he was able to sign out and go home.

His phone chimed, and he almost knocked his chair over getting to it. He sneaked out of the van and jogged to the corner where Poe was waiting.

"You wore black." He was disappointed the little man didn't have yellow on again. Yellow was a happy color.

"I didn't know what was appropriate for a stakeout."

"I'm glad you came. Let's get to the van. The guy seems to have tucked in for the night."

He took a chance and laced his fingers through Poe's. Poe's hand was soft and warm, and he wondered what it would feel like on his chest, stomach, wrapped around his cock. Sex ruined things. No one ever decided to keep him after they fucked. He cussed himself as he quickly led Poe down the street. He opened the back door, wrapped his hands around Poe's sides and his fingers sunk into the softness, he nearly groaned. He loved soft. Soft was good.

He got the little man inside, stepped up behind him and eased the door closed. He noticed Poe checking all the pictures taped to one of the walls.

"Who are they?"

"I'll tell you while we eat."

Poe went with burgers and fries; he was glad it wasn't fancy.

"Pick one." He motioned toward the wall.

Poe studied the wall for a minute and pointed to one of him and Lily the first Christmas he'd spent with the Trenton family.

"That's Lily."

"That's the *when all else fails, a shovel and lye, son*. She doesn't look the type. She looks…sweet."

"She is. We have talks at night, and she rubs my head, tells me I'm one of her kids."

"How did you meet her?"

"I went to get some ink done at Twirled several years ago, and I met her son Lucky, he looked at me and said, *My mom will fucking love you. You're coming home with me.* I thought he was joking because Lucky is kinda crazy. But he took me to his mom and dad's place. She fed me. Told me I was spending the night because she wasn't ready to let me go yet."

"It sounds really nice."

"It was weird…no one ever wanted to keep me before." He cleared his throat as he realized what he'd said and turned to stare at the wall that was covered with the people he considered family.

"I know him." Poe pointed to the picture of Liv. "Who's the man beside him?"

"Fielding. That's Liv's boy. They got married last year."

"I pictured someone more…I don't know, like him. Big and masculine."

30

He liked that Poe didn't mention Liv's scars and that pretty Fielding didn't match Liv.

"Oh, he's working on getting him bigger, that man is obsessed with his boy's belly. And Fielding likes making his daddy happy."

"Daddy?"

He noticed Poe's look and snorted. "You have no idea, you've never heard anything as disturbing as Fielding yelling, *Daddy, fuck me*, as loud as he can from Livingston's office. Um, I shouldn't have said that, sorry."

He forced himself to look away from Poe's face that was red with embarrassment and continued eating.

"You don't talk about yourself much, why?"

"I'm not that interesting."

"A man who kidnaps someone because he felt five rapid to the gut has to be interesting."

"I'm really sorry about that. I don't always think before I act and it gets me in trouble."

"What did the five rapid to the gut mean?"

He wondered if he should tell Poe about Lily and his conversation. Even though he wanted to keep Poe, maybe it was best to let the pretty man know he was damaged.

"I was talking to Lily the night before, and she told me about when she met Damon. Said it was like being struck by lightning and she knew when I met my person it would be the same. When I saw you it—I was wrong, and I shouldn't have done that." The lie barely made it past his lips.

"It's really okay. It was kinda nice to be considered someone's person even if it got me kidnapped. My life is pretty boring, so it broke the monotony."

Poe looked a bit sad for a minute, and he wanted that full, open smile aimed at him again.

"Glad I could help."

"Tell me all the stories before I have to go home and get ready for work."

And he did because he wanted to see Poe happy. It was odd to think about other people, but this wasn't like his friends or family, this was the man he'd—for a brief moment—thought of as his person. He spent hours telling stories until the sun started to rise and he pulled away from the curb, he stopped beside Poe's car, and the man started to get out. He needed just one. He grabbed Poe's arm and pulled the smaller man to the side until his lips brushed against Poe's. He groaned at the softness—everything about Poe was soft, and he craved it.

"Thanks for hanging out with me."

Poe kept staring at his mouth. "You're welcome. Go home and get some sleep."

"What about you?"

"I don't sleep a lot. I'll be fine."

He reluctantly let Poe get out of his van and waited until Poe was in his vehicle. He drove off and headed home. His place was his sanctuary, but now he wanted Poe in his bed when he returned home from work. The night after Poe left his warehouse he'd awakened hard and reached out for his little man. He'd done it for a faceless person most times he opened his eyes, but they'd always been a specter. But not since he'd met Poe. And it hurt as much as it had for the last seventeen years, yet this time was different—Poe actually seemed to like him. They all seemed to like him before they got what they wanted from him. If he desired to keep Poe, he'd have to keep it in his pants.

NO PAIN, NO GAIN

*E*very muscle in his body burned and the pain was close to a level he couldn't bear. Still he pushed. He paid for a private trainer so that he could get a man. At twenty-nine, he was lonely, and he grew tired of being just some *in the dark* fuck. His ass was good enough when he was bent over. The last man he'd slept with was two years ago when his sister had set him up on a blind date with a man she worked with and had appeared nice. Seemed interested in what he had to say.

"Focus, you want that gut gone. Another set of ten."

The trainer's hands were too tight, almost bruising around his biceps as the man pushed him to lift the weights. He struggled too hard, and he flinched as he felt twinges in his shoulders.

"If you're not going to take this seriously, you can—"

"If you don't get your hands off him right now, I'll bury you."

He flinched at the anger in Harmon's voice, and he opened his eyes to find the trainer backing away. Harmon approached him and easily removed the weights from his hands, dropping them to the floor with a loud clang.

"He wants to lose weight. He has to focus. He's thirty pounds overweight for his—"

"He's fucking perfect is what he is."

"Little, what the fuck is going on?" Livingston came up behind Harmon, but Harmon ignored the other man.

Gentle hands helped him to sit up and then eased him to his feet. Harmon worked his shoulders, and he whimpered at the soreness of his muscles, but Harmon's touch felt so good. He didn't know what it was about Harmon, but since the man kidnapped him, he couldn't stop thinking about Harmon. The odd sweetness of the adorable man should've turned out to be impossible, but that's exactly what Harmon was. He wanted Harmon, and he knew it was impossible. The fact of that saddened him. Yet, there wasn't anything he could do about that.

"This fucker was making Poe lift more than he should."

"Stu, is that right? You mistreating your client?"

"If he wants a six-pack, he'll do the work-out my way."

His face flamed and he lowered his gaze to Harmon's bare chest. Sweat beaded in the curly hair and he had an uncontrollable urge to lean in to stroke his cheeks over the sleek skin and hair, just to find out if the hair was coarse or soft. He wanted to trace the lines on the skull that covered the front of Harmon's throat with his tongue. Hell, he just wanted to lick Harmon.

"You want a six-pack?"

"Men like—"

"Not all men," Harmon whispered as he stroked the back of his fingers across his cotton covered belly and pushed slightly into the jiggly curve. "Soft, I love soft."

He glanced up to catch Harmon staring at his belly and where Harmon's fingers rubbed in slow circles. That's when he noticed the manly scent of sweat, a hint of something smoky and spicy. It was the same scent he'd taken in while they were in Harmon's van a week before. He felt his dick start to react to Harmon's closeness and the heat of his body, so he closed his eyes to think about anything other than climbing Harmon.

"Do you want to lose weight, Poe?"

"Yes, no, I just wanted someone to like me." He didn't know why he admitted that, but for some reason, he didn't want to lie to Harmon.

"If someone doesn't like you as is, baby, they ain't worth your time. You shouldn't hurt yourself, and that fucker should've known better. I saw the pain on your face from across the room."

Harmon's tone turned colder, and it sounded more dangerous than the rage of before. He needed to distract Harmon from getting himself into trouble.

"What are you doing here? I didn't know you worked out here."

"I don't. We teach a self-defense class for abuse survivors once a week. Oh, you can meet Fielding."

He couldn't help smiling as Harmon jerked his head around and called over a man a few inches taller than him, well, average height for a man. He'd always been in the lower percentile for growth until he hit puberty and he'd gained weight instead of height.

"This is Fielding."

Seeing the beautiful blond in person was different, the man's pictures didn't do him justice at all, and he realized the man was familiar. "You're Fielding Hask—"

"Livingston now."

"Weren't you going to do some big blockbuster a year ago?"

"I found something more important." Fielding's smile was so sweet as the man's big husband wrapped his arms around his thick waist.

"I told you that you could still do your acting if you wanted."

"I know, Daddy, but that meant I couldn't sleep in your arms every night and that wasn't happening."

The love between those two men was awe-inspiring. Livingston was big and muscular, and Fielding was slim and beautiful even with the slight belly.

"Do you want to go to lunch with us," Harmon asked. "We're just hitting the diner."

"Are you getting dressed first?" he asked and let his eyes scan all that muscled perfection.

Huge, hairy pectorals flexed, and he grinned at Harmon's chuckle.

"If I keep getting looked at like that, I might leave the shirt off."

"Put the shirt on, Harmon." His voice was strained at thinking of other people looking at him.

"Yes, Poe."

No one ever called him Poe, it was always Solomon or Solo as a joke. His sister always called him Solo because that's what he always said when she asked him if he was bringing anyone to family dinner or events she invited him to. His parents loved him, but they were outgoing and athletic, running marathons.

Harmon slipped his shirt over his head, and he regretted making Harmon put clothes on. He missed that dark skin and hair instantly.

"We have another thirty minutes to work out."

He turned his attention back to Stu and took in the man's annoyed expression.

"No, the work-out is done, and if he wants to work-out, he can ask me to train him. I'm not letting you anywhere near him."

"You'd train me?"

"You can come out to my place—"

A gasp cut Harmon off, and he peeked around the big man to see Fielding's eyes wide.

"You're going to let someone come to your place? *Your place?*"

"Why can't I go to his place?"

"Little won't even let most people know his address. I think four people know where he lives and no one but Lily dares go over there."

"He's got a nice place."

"Your person, Little?"

He held his breath as he waited for the answer. Would Harmon say he was his person? He knew it would never work, but he really wanted to be—

"He's a friend."

He turned away and bent over to grab his bag to hide the hurt he knew was on his face. He didn't want to embarrass himself in front of Harmon and the man's friends.

"Come on, let's go get some food," Livingston ordered.

He straightened as Livingston dragged Fielding toward the door.

"If you don't want to have lunch with us, that's okay."

"No, I want to, but if you don't want me to come…"

"I do," Harmon said too loud and sharp. "Sorry, my friends are weird sometimes."

"You did tell me all those stories, so, I kinda got that."

"Here, let me take your bag." Harmon plucked the backpack from his hold.

A big hand rested on his lower back and nudged him forward. He let Harmon lead him in the direction of the door, and Harmon grabbed a small gym bag that Fielding held out to him.

"You okay with walking? We left our cars at the office."

"A walk is fine," he answered as they followed Livingston and Fielding.

The two men held hands and talked softly to each other.

"How did Livingston and Fielding meet? I don't think that was one of the stories."

"Fielding had a stalker, and a guy in L.A. who knew Linus, recommended us. Livingston was assigned as a bodyguard for Fielding."

"So they fell in love?"

"Yeah, Livingston was going to let Fielding go after the assignment was over. Didn't think it was fair to tie Fielding to him. Liv kept it up right until Fielding was about to get on the plane. He couldn't let his boy go."

"And they got married?"

"Several months ago."

"I never thought about getting married, no, that's not true, I've thought about it, but it just never seemed like it was meant to be."

"You're still young, what twenty-three, four?"

"I'm thirty in a few months."

"I didn't expect that."

"Yeah, I've always looked a lot younger than I am. It's a curse."

"No, it's not. You're very beautiful."

"Thank you for saying so, but I don't see it."

"You should, and I think I might say it a lot until you believe it."

He couldn't help it, he wrapped his arms around Harmon's and hugged it to his chest. "You're really sweet, Harmon, why are you single?" He felt Harmon flinch and glanced up to find the man's face expressionless.

"No one wants to keep me for more than one fuck."

"That's bullshit. Any person would be lucky to have you."

"You'd be in a minority of one."

He was about to argue when he noticed Harmon was no longer looking at him. There was an oppressive sadness that seemed to weigh Harmon down. He'd noticed it. Just small details, when Harmon told Lily that he didn't like Harmon much. When Harmon hadn't wanted to let go of his hand. And in the van when Harmon said no one ever wanted to keep him.

He'd admit Harmon was a bit out there, but he'd love a chance at keeping the weirdly adorable man. Unfortunately, Harmon was determined that he was only a friend. He didn't have time to say anything before Harmon ushered him into the diner. Harmon motioned him onto the bench seat of the booth first, same as Livingston did with Fielding.

"Little, Liv, Fielding, what are you three doing here during the day?"

"Just finished at the gym. This is Little's friend, Poe. This is the beautiful Heidi." Fielding answered as the man leaned into his husband's side.

"Hi, Poe, I've seen you in here a few times. How did you hook up with these heathens?"

"Harmon kidnapped me."

She just laughed and shook her head. "I can see him doing it. What can I get y'all to drink? Your usual apple juice, Little?"

"Yes, ma'am."

Heidi took their drink orders and left them menus. When she came back, he ordered a burger and fries like the rest of them. It would be the first real food he'd had since he'd taken Harmon dinner on the stakeout. While they waited for their food, Harmon stretched his arm out along the top of the booth seat, and he took a chance. He settled into Harmon's side, and the big man seemed to relax at his weight. It was nice, and he enjoyed lunch with people he might be able to see as friends. Although, he didn't want to be just friends with Harmon, he'd deal with it just to be able to be with him. The man made him feel good for the first time in a long while.

WHEN HAD HARMON LAST HUNG OUT WITH A MAN: NEVER

*H*e ran around the house, and then he'd rolled a blunt and was trying to bring his nerves under control. Poe had called him that morning and asked him if he wanted to hang out. He never hung out with a man before, well, his friends but that was different. This was a man he liked a lot. They'd talked and exchanged messages because he'd worked nights and Poe mostly days. It wasn't much but something. They'd even gotten together at the diner at least once a week in the past month.

After the gym incident, he'd made the personal trainer's life hell. A smirk tugged at the corner of his mouth. The man barely had any clients left and not to mention the fucker's girlfriend found out about his other girlfriend and wife. He didn't believe monogamy was a default setting. As long as it was agreed to, that was different. The man deserved to get knocked down from his throne. Those people who thought they were better than everyone else because of status or body fat pissed him off.

He finished throwing all his dirty laundry in front of the washer and dryer at the back of the warehouse. He had to write it on his board of things to do. Being stuck on cheating spouse duty made him lazy. He liked his job, loved it most of the time, but he hated when he was cooped up in the back of his van for too long. The walls started to close in around him.

The buzzer went off. Shit, Poe was early. He jogged across the expanse of the first floor and slammed his hand onto the button for the doors. He stepped forward and held his breath as he'd never felt such disappointment when he noticed it wasn't Poe.

"Little, man, ya gotta help me."

"What did you do to Fielding?"

"Nothing, my boy is fine, we're fine. Give me that," Livingston growled as he passed him and grabbed the blunt.

Liv rarely smoked with him, must be something big.

"If you and your boy are good, why the fuck are you smoking then?"

"Fielding thinks it's time for a pet."

He bit his lip to keep from laughing as he followed Liv to the living-slash-kitchen area. He cringed as his couch creaked when the big man fell onto it. He *really* needed to get new furniture, especially now that he had a man friend. He couldn't call Poe his boyfriend. Did the man even want to be his boyfriend? *Shit, don't think about it.*

"Dude, you two are married, he didn't ask for you to breed, so I don't know why you're panicking about a pet."

He stole the blunt back and took a seat in his favorite recliner.

"We already had the kid talk. I'm too old and selfish. I love having Fielding to myself."

Livingston being a dad, he couldn't see it. Not that the man wouldn't be a good one, but Liv didn't want to share Fielding. "You two talked about kids?"

"Don't sound so fucking shocked. It's not like our friends don't have kids. It was logical as fuck to have the conversation."

"I see this was an issue." He stopped a smile from forming by taking another hit as Liv sent him a very clear *I'll kill you* look.

"It's not an issue," Liv growled.

"Did you want kids, Liv?"

"No, absolutely not. Like I said I'm selfish, but Fielding's young, he might change his mind and aren't pets like test runs to see if you can keep a mini carbon-based life form alive?"

"Sometimes people just want pets." He took a deep inhale and held it, then exhaled as he talked. "Fielding wasn't allowed things. Maybe he always wanted one, and since he's happily married to your cranky ass, he's ready." He placed the rest of his blunt in the ashtray for later. He didn't want to be too messed up when Poe got there. He'd needed to take the edge off his anxiety.

"I'm still trying to get my head around the fact that boy of mine agreed to marry me."

He watched as Liv leaned forward to rest his forearms on his knees. The two men were so perfect for each other. He knew Liv was self-conscious with his background and the amount of scarring on his face and body. It didn't matter how badass the guy was, shit like that bothered a person.

"You're lucky, man, why fucking question it?"

"He's in his early twenties, beautiful, and here I am old and scarred."

"Don't do that shit, Liv. Everybody who sees how he looks at you knows Fielding loves you."

"It's just so much, like too much too soon I guess. I'm just waiting for all that shit to explode in my face."

"It won't, man. You two are in it for good. So, what kinda pet does—"

"Hi. You left your door open. Hope you don't mind I came on in."

He spun around as he saw Poe standing there in jeans and a yellow t-shirt. He was slightly disappointed Poe wasn't wearing a bow tie. But he noticed one thing Poe always wore something in his favorite color. Poe remembered the details and more than anything those small things made him feel important.

"No, hi, shit." He stood up and offered his chair to Poe. He

43

froze as the man gave him a quick hug around his waist and took a seat in the recliner.

"I saw Livingston's bike. I figured you had company. I'm not interrupting some work thing, am I?"

He lowered himself to the floor to sit beside Poe's legs, "No, Liv's boy wants a pet."

He tried not to look like an idiot when Poe draped an arm around him and kissed the top of his head. Poe touched him a lot. It wasn't anything sexual. He held his hand. Hugged him. No one had touched him so much in his life, not even Lily who was super affectionate with him.

"Pets are great. What kind does he want?"

"Don't know, he just mentioned it when I called him at lunch, and I said we could discuss it when I got home."

"Discuss means Fielding will ask, but Daddy always has the final say." He raised his hand to cover his mouth when Liv gave him the death glare. The man was a professional at it.

"You know, it wouldn't hurt my feelings to kill you."

"Then I wouldn't have to listen to you fucking your boy while we try to talk about work."

"Not my fault you call when I'm having a moment with my boy."

Poe's musical laughter came from behind him, and he felt the man shaking with it.

"I find your exhibitionism disturbing."

He'd gone out to Liv's place too many times since his friend married Fielding to find them fucking outside. They didn't even stop. If he had a man of his own, he wouldn't let anyone see his man like that, but people got off on stuff. Wasn't his place to judge.

"It is what it is, man."

"You came here asking for help. What did you want help with?"

"Nothing, just killing some time before I gotta go home."

He chuckled. "The big, bad death junkie is hiding from his cute husband."

Liv shook his head and sighed heavily. "When he bats his lashes and calls me Daddy I can't tell him no."

"Completely whipped."

Liv nodded toward Poe and smirked. "You'll know what it's like one day. I'll let you get to your date."

He stayed seated as Liv got up and headed for the door. Poe called out a goodbye, and Liv waved over his shoulder.

"I hope I didn't ruin your talk with Liv." Poe squeezed him and pressed a kiss below his ear.

"No, he really did come to avoid going home for a few."

He didn't even know if Poe noticed all the touching, but he couldn't ignore the hands rubbing his chest as they talked.

"Fielding doesn't look all that scary."

"He's not, but Liv is a control freak, and he can't tell Fielding no."

"I think it's sweet."

He groaned. "Don't ever let Liv hear you say he's sweet."

"I will refrain."

He turned his head to look up at Poe, and he froze as Poe lowered his mouth to his. It was a soft brush. There wasn't a push for deeper or more.

"So, what are we going to do tonight?"

He loved the warm rush of Poe's breath across his mouth. He raised his hand to stroke the back of his fingers along the soft skin of the man's cheek. Poe leaned into his touch and seemed to relax. In all his thirty-two years, no one had ever reacted to him the way Poe had. He would've sworn Poe would hate him after he'd displayed his embarrassing lack of impulse control.

"I thought we could take a ride to go get some takeout and come back here, watch a movie or play a game."

"I've never played video games before."

He was sure he looked horrified. What person hadn't played

video games? What the hell had Poe done growing up? Read? "Are you joking right now?"

A smile spread the corners of Poe's mouth wide. "No, I'm not joking."

"We really have to change that." He pushed to his feet and grabbed Poe's hands. "What do you want for dinner?"

"What's the quickest and easiest? I got busy today and forgot to have lunch."

"There's a few fast food places."

"You're on. I require grease and fat."

"Whatever you want."

They hopped into his van, and he drove down to the highway, then to the nearest fast food place. He could've probably left Poe at his place, but when he was with Poe, he didn't want to be away from him. Even after a few months of friendship, he still wasn't secure that he'd have Poe around for long. He ordered and pulled around, then he took the bags and handed them to Poe.

"Do you always eat this much?"

"I'm a growing boy." He winked at Poe and noticed the man raked his gaze over him.

His dick liked that once over too much. He was determined to keep it friendly between them. His past experiences proved that he wasn't the man that people looked at as their forever. Since Poe had come along, he spent every night jerking off to fantasies of what Poe would do to him. They kept him sane when he lay in his lonely bed and imagined what it would be like to have Poe there.

He thought about the sex, but it was more than that. He lived a perfect fantasy life in his head, and it included the everyday things like shared meals, cuddling, and being a couple. He liked sex well enough. It served a purpose to take the edge off or let him pretend he belonged to someone. But other than momentary release, when the afterglow faded, he was back to choking on his loneliness. Platonic with Poe was so much more important than some meaningless fuck.

In record time he had them back at the warehouse and parked in front of the TV waiting for the game to start.

They ate and laughed. He learned more about Poe but avoided personal questions about himself. He didn't like his past. There wasn't much to be proud of hidden in the experiences he had or the choices he'd made. Surviving and living were two separate entities fused and cloaked only in their similarities.

He froze as Poe hooked his right leg over his left and sat close as he told him what all the buttons on the controllers were for, then they started to play a new shooter game. Poe sucked at it.

"You shot me!" Poe screeched as he nudged him with his shoulder.

The shove barely made him move, and he paused the game. "Dude, you ran in front of me while I was firing, of course I was going to shoot you. Next, I'll use you as a shield."

"Harmon, I'm so not feeling the love right now. Start the game over."

"I'm winning, why would I—"

"Don't make me take you out."

Poe had the cutest glare on his face like an angry puppy. "Fuck, you're so cute when you're mad."

Why did Poe being irritated or angry make his cock take notice? He wanted to lean forward and kiss him in a very not friend-like way. He'd never wanted a man on his dick more than he did right then.

"I'm not cute. I'm dangerous."

He sucked his lips between his teeth and bit down hard to keep from laughing at Poe's expression. He was pretty sure it was supposed to be badass, but it wasn't.

"Why are you laughing?"

"I'm not laughing."

"You're lying," Poe said with a growl and attacked.

He found himself pushed flat onto the couch and Poe too quickly discovered he was ticklish. Useless, he was fucking useless when someone tickled him, and he kept it a secret. He laughed and yelled for Poe to stop as he tried to protect his ribs. Although, he was careful not to push Poe off just in case the man hurt himself. He couldn't live with that, accident or not.

"Say I win, Harmon, say it," Poe ordered.

"No, no surrender."

Poe got him under his arms and without thinking he spun until Poe was beneath him. They were both breathing heavily as they looked at each other.

"I now know your weakness…I will be unstoppable."

"You'd use my weakness against me?" He pouted and tried to pretend that being between Poe's thighs wasn't affecting him. The softness of Poe's belly conformed to the hard plane of his own. Everything about the man seemed to be made for him, and it was so hard to deny himself. Fear and self-preservation were stronger than his need for a physical relationship with Poe.

An evil smirk tilted the corner of Poe's mouth. "In a heartbeat. Can we just watch a movie? I don't think I'm cut out for video games."

"Can do, what do you want to watch? I've been wanting to do a *Hellraiser* marathon."

Poe rolled his beautiful blue eyes. "Of course you'd like gore-fest movies."

"So good, so, ya wanna?" He waggled his brows, and when Poe pushed against his chest, he rose to his knees.

"Bring on *Pinhead* and the *Cenobites*."

He crawled onto the floor toward his collection of DVDs, most of his movies were digital, but he had some favorites on disk. He ejected the game from the console and loaded the first movie.

"If you don't like horror, how do you know the characters?"

"I didn't say I didn't like it, big guy, I just remarked that of course you'd like gory movies."

"I have a lot of interests besides gory movies."

"Yes, lethal amounts of energy drinks. A strange obsession with apple juice."

"Hey, apple juice is healthy, unlike all those sodas you like to drink." He pointed to the tub of soft drink Poe was currently hugging to his chest.

"Helluva lot better than your heart attack in a can."

"Blah, blah, blah." He crawled back on the couch as Poe curled up against his side and he started the movie, then threw the controller aside. He leaned forward and grabbed the last of his blunt. "You mind?"

"You do you, man."

He rolled his eyes as he lit it and relaxed to watch the movie with Poe. He savored the contentment of being with Poe. The novelty of how nice it was to just be him with someone didn't pass unnoticed. He liked that. He wanted to keep it as long as he could and knew exactly what he needed to do. Keep it in his pants.

HARMON WAS SO SWEET

*H*e laughed to himself as he remembered the last four nights he'd spent at Harmon's place. The video games he could do without. He'd discovered quickly he wasn't good at them and Harmon was vicious as hell. Although, the cuddling after Harmon kicked his ass were the highlights of his evenings. They'd finally released Harmon from cheating spouse duty, and the man had to go out of town for a few days.

The distance between them wasn't something he was looking forward to, but Harmon promised to call at least once a day. He didn't know what the man was going to be doing and he hoped he wouldn't be a distraction.

Harmon promised when he returned he was going to take him to meet the rest of his friends. He'd heard so many stories that it was weird he hadn't met the Trenton Crew or Lily yet. He hadn't met many people since moving to Powers. Working from home blurred most of his days into one, and before Harmon came along, he barely paid attention to the passing of time except when he needed to head to the city to work.

That had also gone by the wayside a bit too. He'd called in and said he had to work from home. His remote job didn't require him to go to the office at all. The only reason to go to Atlanta was if he needed to do some hands-on research. Clients were more than happy to have meetings over the phone.

Today, though, he had plans, a trip to Well Loved Thrift was in order. The owner of the place called to say she'd gotten a consignment of funky bow ties in a few days earlier from an online client. So, he'd do a bit of shopping and then go to lunch before coming home to work some more.

He thought it was time for him to stock up on some new ties. He didn't miss Harmon's disappointment when he showed up not wearing a bow tie. People always thought his obsession was odd, but Harmon seemed to love them. The fact he loved making the man happy even if it was something as small as wearing a tie hadn't escaped him. The simple things made Harmon content. He knew every one from the way Harmon reacted. Harmon would relax into a hug. Would hold him as if he gave the man a rare gift just by touching him.

Okay, Harmon was gorgeous from his dark hair to the tips of his tactical boots, but he was much more than his looks, he was the sweetest man he'd ever met.

He closed down his laptop and pushed away from his desk. The walk to Well Loved would give him a bit of exercise. He hadn't gone back to the gym. Yes, he thought he needed to get up from his desk more, but he'd always been on the chunky side. Nothing he'd done for the month he'd worked out had made any difference in his size.

Harmon had been right, if someone didn't like him, then that was their problem. He ate healthily. His weakness for fast food once a week wasn't the worst thing in the world. He tried to walk at least three times a week. Happiness and contentment were his only goals and torturing himself wasn't going to get him those.

He locked and closed his front door and headed toward the thrift store. He liked to shop, and it helped him think, retail therapy was real and he was proof.

Harmon was interested. He knew the man wanted more than what they had going, but something was holding him back. As much as he wanted to possibly move from platonic to a romantic relationship, he loved having Harmon as a friend. He was fun and didn't take everything so seriously.

Again, he wasn't too crazy about Harmon's job, but he wouldn't complain. Harmon had told too many stories of close calls for his comfort. He could deal with it.

If he made eye contact with anyone on his walk, he was polite and said hello, but he wasn't much of a people person. His parents didn't pass on the sociable gene to him like they had his sister. His family was the type of people who had never met a stranger. They were so weird.

He finally made it to the store, and he pulled open the door, walking into vintage heaven.

"My Goddess of Vintage Apparel, what shall you gift me with today?" he asked as he approached the counter and the pretty woman behind it.

Grace was a semi-new resident like him. She'd moved to town and bought Well Loved from the elderly former owner. Nothing much had changed around the store except Grace had put her own funky spin on things. It was like a messy mix of the decades between the 20s and 70s. She ran an online site where she sold her more rare and expensive finds.

"I shall gift to you a shit ton of silk bow ties that look like someone on LSD designed them."

"You had my interest at silk but hooked me at acid tripping designer."

He grinned at her husky laugh and followed as she pointed for him to go toward the back.

"Weirdo. So, what's new? Last time you graced me with your fashionable presence you were torturing yourself."

She took his arm, and they squeezed through the narrow

rows, and she rested her head on his shoulder. She was chunky like him and just about the same height.

"Alas, I had to let the sadist go."

She pouted and sighed. "Shame, hard to find a good sadist these days."

"Got something to tell me?"

"No, the only thing interesting about me is my shop. I think I exercised once and it was the worse two minutes of my life. One cramp and I was done."

"My new friend offered to train me if I wanted him to."

"New friend? Mysterious. Do tell me more."

He pulled out his phone and scrolled to the picture he'd taken of Harmon the other night while he worked out. "I supervised his work-out a few days ago. I do love my job." He held the phone out.

"All that is unholy, I'm jealous. Where did you meet, and does he have a hot brother, friend, hell, distant cousin?"

"We kinda ran into each other in the grocery store a few months back. Started hanging out, but we're just friends."

"Friends isn't always a bad thing."

"I know, but I want to put boy beside that friend. I think he's had some bad experiences, so I'm happy being friends."

She spun away from him as they reached the back storage room and faced him. Her expression turned solemn as she placed her hands in front of her in prayer position. "Now, I will show you the beauty of the ages, the Gods of Geekdom have blessed us. Behold, the epic bow ties." She motioned toward the box with a flourish and a bow.

He giggled at the impish grin on her face. Some would say Grace was a plain woman, but when she smiled, she could make the most classically beautiful woman envious.

He approached the box and looked into it, and he knew love at first sight. It was as if every color known to humankind had thrown up in explosions of paisley and gloriously ugly designs. It was Nirvana in a box.

"Be at ease, my friend, take in the glory of our bounty."

"Why are you single, Grace?"

She shrugged. "I don't know, just haven't met the right person yet."

The happiness on her face dimmed a bit, but not by much. "Well, I must have all the ones with even a hint of yellow in them."

"That's almost the entire box. Even you, obsessor of bow ties, don't need that many."

"Yes, I need them. Plus, Harmon's favorite color is yellow, and I make sure to wear it every time I see him. It makes him happy."

She let out a long sigh and slumped against his side. "That's so sweet."

"Not as sweet as he is and it's a tiny thing I can do."

"Does no one work in this store, every time I come here I have to search for a sale's person," A good-naturedly annoyed voice came from the door.

He turned to find Harper, the owner of the local bookstore lazing in the doorway. Grace and Harper were best friends and had been close for a few years before Grace had moved to Powers.

"I don't work here, so, don't blame me."

"Hey, Harper, don't have your shadow today?"

"Gideon is at home and decided to keep Ricky for a father/daughter day. So, I'm in need of a lunch companion or two. And Solomon, since we've run into each other today, I heard this very interesting rumor."

"Do tell, you know I'm out of the loop of gossip with my hermit ways."

He turned to peer into the mass of ties. He picked through the box and even a hint of yellow he snatched it up. He even found one that was solid yellow with silver pinstripes. He had a gray shirt that would be perfect with it.

"You're seeing a certain Trenton employee, and he gets all shy and blushy when he talks about you."

He knew he wore a goofy grin thinking that Harmon was all shy when he talked about him. It proved the man liked him and he needed to be patient with him.

"You know Harmon? But to clear it up, we're hanging out as friends."

"Whatever you say, Harmon is not thinking just friends. I've known him for years. Little hangs out with the Crews, so, he comes around quite a bit. All the Crews are pretty tight, and Trenton's crew helped me out a while back."

Powers wasn't a terribly small place, and gossip was a pastime around there, but each part of Powers had its own brand of gossip. But in the center, you heard it all. It was one of the reasons he knew that Harper had a violent ex and he'd tried to kill her and her now husband, Gideon. He'd experienced some wariness when he'd thought about moving here. The old Sheriff had turned out to be a rampant homophobe and racist, but, luckily, the new one, Pelter, didn't stand for either of those things.

"Would you like to join me and Grace for lunch, and maybe I can tell you a few stories."

He spun around with about twenty bow ties in his hands and grinned at Harper. "You got info on what the man likes to eat or his interests?"

"I could possibly assist you, for a price?" Harper's voice was Godfather-esque, and she buffed her nails on the cotton of her dress, then looked at them.

"A steep price?"

"It'll cost you pie with extra ice cream."

He gasped. "Shit, extra ice cream?"

"Wait too long, and it'll cost ya extra, extra ice cream."

"Whoa, whoa, no need to get bloodthirsty, you got a deal."

"And excuse me, I'm supposed to be your best friend after Gideon, and I don't get introduced to the hot guys or treated to gossip about hot guys?"

"You bit your tongue and choked on your own spit when we tried to hook you up on a date. I thought you were, dead, dead, my friend. I will not be responsible for that."

"He looked like some male model who would be on a damn magazine cover."

"Sorry, should I not introduce you to sweet, hot, tattooed bikers?"

"Yes, but warn me next time."

He shook his head and left them to argue as he carried his ties to the front. "How much am I charging myself?" he yelled.

"What did I charge last time?" Grace asked as she approached with Harper behind her.

"I don't remember. You gave me some weird friends and family discount. I believe there were letters and weird Sanskrit symbols in the math."

"Get out of there."

He covered his head as she playfully batted at him and he ran from behind the counter. He leaned on the surface as Harper came up beside him. Her slight weight was leaning into his side.

"She needs a boyfriend or more shopping trips to Pleasure."

"I think Sin and Saint put up a Be on the Watch for Grace sign in front of the store a few months ago."

Sin and Saint Pelter were married to the Sheriff, and they had a beautiful little girl. He couldn't think about one unhappy couple he'd met since he'd moved here. He was sure they had their problems like everyone else, but you could feel the love radiating from them.

"Those little shits, if they didn't run so damn fast they'd be dead. Anybody walking past or going inside would think I was a nympho."

He laughed as Grace huffed and shook her head.

"Last I heard you had to have sex to be a nympho."

He quickly covered his mouth to contain his laughter at Grace's horrified expression.

"You're just on it today, Harper Jane, ha, ha, ha."

He observed the interplay between the two women. He'd always liked them both, but he'd never been one to make friends easily. When he was able to spend time with them, he had a blast. He worked too much and hadn't realized how much he seemed to be missing out on until Harmon's arrival made him take stock of his life.

He had Harmon now, people he considered friends, and all it took was getting kidnapped by an adorable man with poor impulse control.

Grace announced his total, and he paid with his card. "So, ladies, will we be dining at the local diner for lunch?" He put his card back in his wallet and took the bag with his new pretties.

"We need sustenance." They both grabbed his arms and dragged him to the door.

"Now, let's see if we can get you out of the friend zone," Harper said as she squeezed his arm.

He would do just about anything to get Harmon to date him. He wanted to be Harmon's person.

SO BEAUTIFUL

he heavy bag swung wildly as he landed punches and tried to clear his mind. His life had changed so much since he'd met Poe and still it was the same. The man was so beautiful and all he wanted to do was touch him every time he saw Poe. His cock hardened when he was with the small man. Sex always ruined everything. No matter how much he wanted to love on Poe, he resisted so that he could just spend time.

"What did that bag do to you?" Lily's voice amused as she asked.

"I met my person."

"I know, you called me remember?"

"I told him I was wrong and we were just friends." He hugged the bag and rested his forehead on it.

"Why the fuck would you do that, Harmon?"

Lily wrapped her small hands around his sides and turned him to face her. He avoided meeting her gaze because he didn't want to see her disappointment.

"Because sex ruins everything and I don't want him to get tired of me."

"Harmon, you look at me, and you don't lie to me. You know the Trenton rules."

"I'm not a Trenton."

He grunted as a small fist connected with his stomach.

"I'm sorry."

"You never say that to me again, Harmon. I may not have birthed your oversized ass, but you're my son. Just like with the rest of my fucked-up kids. I ain't like Peaches, and I ain't all eloquent and shit like her. I know bad things happened to you before you came to be mine. You were used and discarded."

He let her lead him to his chair and push him into it; then she sat on his lap.

"Fucking is amazing, visceral and nasty, but what you lack, my son, is intimacy. You've never had intimacy."

"What's the difference?"

He was always someone's one-night stand. He knew he wasn't handsome. He tended to say and do the wrong thing, and he fell so easily for a moment of affection.

"Lucky and Priest had a lot of intimacy before they began a sexual relationship. Intimacy is about touch. Kisses. Allowing yourself to be naked not only physically, but emotionally with someone else. You don't have to touch someone's pussy or cock to be physical with someone. It's embraces, kisses, and touching. Anyone can fuck, Harmon."

"He's beautiful, Lily. He's soft and sweet. Poe wears these cute little bow ties and glasses. I just want to touch him when I see him."

"Why don't you ask your young man on a date?"

He thought about lying but knew it wouldn't fly with Lily. She had a radical honesty philosophy. "I don't want him to know how much of a fuck up I am."

"You're not a fuck up, Harmon. You know I can't lie, not even to save your feelings."

"The last man I fucked used me to get to one of my best

friend's boys. He was disgusted by me. Thought I was the weakest link in the team. I was always just the fuck, never the boyfriend. I was thirteen when I lost my virginity, and someone paid me for it."

Lily's soft hands took his face and forced him to look at her. "You did things to survive. There's not a lot of ways to make your way on the streets. You have to eat. Put a roof over your head. Those men and women who paid you for your body were wrong in what they did. You were a child. I don't care how tall you were or how old you looked. They committed a crime."

"I just wanted to be allowed to touch, Lily. Just hold someone and pretend they were mine. The tricks weren't always at fault."

She kissed his right cheek then the other—brushed her lips to his lashes.

"Your biological mother left you. From what you've told me about what you can remember you weren't even allowed the most basic affection." Lily brushed a kiss to his forehead. "You were sent to overfilled foster homes and group homes with overwhelmed staff. You weren't taught appropriate touch." She hugged him tightly around his neck and pressed her lips to his temple. "When your person comes along, they will understand what you need, and you'll have to let them know your limits. A date doesn't need to end in the bedroom or wherever. It's a kiss or hug outside the restaurant or at your date's door."

"I've never done that before."

"Hey, I've never fucked on a space station before, but we all need goals."

He leaned in to sniff her breath for alcohol and arched his brow. "Space station?"

"I know, I know, I think I read an article that men can't get it up in zero gravity, but nothing wrong with my man's tongue."

There was banging on his door, and he shot a panicked look toward it.

"Did anyone follow you?"

"Dude, you know I'm carrying. I made like three U-turns at different turnarounds. Do you think I'm stupid?" He eased her off his lap and stood.

He grabbed the remote off his newly broken coffee table. Lily and him had a bit of an accident the other night. From what he remembered, there was some dancing and some questionable food choices.

He hit the button and listened to the creak of the heavy metal doors. He froze in place as Poe appeared. He was wearing a white dress shirt and a sunny yellow bow tie. He curled his fingers into his palms as the barely controlled urge to touch sent heat infusing his gut.

"You weren't answering your phone, and I got worried."

He didn't know what to say, no one outside of his friends ever worried about him. It was...weird. He cleared his throat and tried to find his voice. "I'm fine."

"Oh my fake baby Jesus, please say I can watch."

He nudged Lily and then wrapped his arm around her shoulders.

"Poe, this is the sweet and always appropriate Lily."

His adorable face brightened, and he stepped inside. "Oh, hi, Harmon has told me so much about you."

"He's so fucking cute. I'll trade you."

The almost maniacal edge to her voice made him nervous, and he held tighter to Lily to keep the woman beside him. Lily in attack mode was going to scare Poe off.

"Thank you, I think."

"My son has told me so much about you. But he didn't say how adorable you were though. Do you smoke?"

"No, but I appreciate the offer."

"They can't all be perfect I guess. I'm going to be headed out. I expect Poe and you for Sunday dinner. No excuses."

He grinned as she grabbed his cheeks and pulled him down

for a kiss. She hugged his neck tight and pressed her lips to his ear.

"I love you, Harmon, more than my own fucked-up biological spawn."

"Love you too, Lily."

"You did good, son." She patted his face.

He rolled his eyes as she grabbed Poe in a tight hug and the man looked ready to panic. Then he noticed she was squeezing Poe's ass.

"Time for you to go."

He picked Lily up by the waist and rescued Poe from the handsy woman. Lily gave him the cutest pout and batted her long blonde lashes at him.

"But just a minute longer, he was starting to like..."

"Bye, Mama."

He laughed as tears filled her eyes and he hit the button to close the doors.

"You called me..."

When the heavy metal doors slid into place blocking Lily, he turned to Poe. The man stood there with a sweet smile curving his mouth, and he wanted to taste the beautiful lines with his tongue. He drove the thoughts away with the memories of all the men and women who came before Poe. He'd finally found the only person he didn't truly want to give up. Sex with Poe would end their time together too soon.

"Wasn't that a bit rude, Harmon?"

"I can open the door and let her rub on you some more."

Poe stepped closer and looked up at him. Poe had his head tilted as if the little man were studying him. "That's quite all right. I made dinner. I left it in the car, would you like to eat with me?"

"I'm going to jump in the shower. Here's the remote." He handed the remote to Poe and let his fingertips brush over Poe's with the exchange.

The man's skin was soft, and the sweetest scent wafted up to him. It was a hint of vanilla with the spiciness of ginger. He almost leaned down to place his nose to Poe's neck just to inhale and memorize it.

"You trust me with the remote for the inner sanctum?"

He reached out to take the remote back, and Poe playfully jumped back, hiding the remote behind him.

"No, no, no, Harmon, go take your shower, and I'll run outside and get dinner. Do you think she's gone?"

"If I know Lily, she's probably still out there with her ear pressed to the door hoping to hear the sounds of sex."

"That's a bit disturbing."

"Why?"

"I don't know. She's your mom."

"She's my friend. The best I ever had."

Lily was like a present he'd never expected. Not only was she his best friend, but she'd also shown him what a mother should be—loving and present. A person without judgment who loved him despite his many failings.

"I can see that. Go get cleaned up."

Poe's soft hands pushed against his chest, and he wanted to lean in and arch his back. Feel Poe's fingers running through the hair on his chest. He had quite a few dreams recently of Poe loving on him—filling him. He hadn't bottomed since he was seventeen and got off the streets with the help of Linus.

The man stepped away too quickly, and he practically jogged to the second floor where his bedroom was. He stripped as his mind went to Poe and that the man would be downstairs waiting for him.

WHAT HAD HE GOTTEN HIMSELF IN TO?

*H*e let himself back into the warehouse and closed the doors behind him. The loud click of the lights that followed his progression wasn't as jarring as it was the first few times he was there. He hoped Harmon liked what he made for dinner. Cooking wasn't his strong suit. His parents always had a cook and housekeeper, and he'd never had to learn to fend for himself.

But there was one thing everyone said he made well. He set out the baking dish of chicken Parmesan, a bowl of salad and a container with breadsticks. With everything on the rickety, 70's style table with cracked corners, he strode to the fridge and pulled out two bottles of apple juice.

His hands tightened around the bottles as Harmon appeared in the kitchen. Harmon wore an unbuttoned white dress shirt and faded low-slung jeans. The man's forearms flexed as Harmon scrubbed a towel over his hair.

"I would've helped."

"No need. I had everything ready. Do you have plates and silverware? I didn't bring those."

"Yeah." Harmon tossed the towel into a clothes basket nearby.

He couldn't resist watching the way Harmon moved. Harmon was graceful and relaxed, like a man who didn't have a care in the world. Harmon didn't rush about.

"I'm curious about you."

"Is that why you brought me dinner…bribes?"

Harmon shot him a grin over his broad shoulder and then turned with plates in hand. "Sit."

He did as Harmon asked and waited. Harmon placed the plates and silverware on the table, then took his own seat. He nearly protested as Harmon started to button his shirt.

"You don't talk much about yourself. You're always asking questions about me or talking about other people. Is there a reason you don't want to tell me?"

"I'm just not all that interesting."

"I don't think that's true. Tell me everything."

"Everything is a lot."

"Start at the beginning, what's your first memory?"

"I think it was my mother leaving me behind at the social services office. I think I may have been five or six."

He wasn't so much horrified by what his mother did but by the lack of emotion in Harmon's voice. His impassive expression as if it hadn't meant anything—that it was expected.

"I'm sorry." He hadn't known what else to say.

"It was a long time ago."

Harmon didn't say anything else as he watched Harmon make his plate first before making one for himself.

"Tell me the good parts. I don't want you sad. How did you come to work for Linus?"

"Long story short, he found out about certain skills that I have, he took advantage of and paid me quite well for them. When I turned eighteen, he hired me on with the old company he worked for before he started his own. I moved here when he started Trenton Security."

That was the most Harmon ever talked about himself, and he

was kind of shocked the big man let that much out. Harmon seemed guarded. From the small amount of information Harmon shared, he'd pieced together that Harmon's life wasn't easy and probably still wasn't. A part of him wanted to make the adorable man happy.

"But you didn't meet Lily until you went to get a tattoo done by Lucky?"

"Yeah, Linus went through this phase where he didn't spend much time with his family. I was always curious because you learn stuff. Sitting around bullshitting with the guys and stories get told. Linus sounded like his family annoyed him, but they seemed downright perfect to me. When Lucky took me to see Lily, I already felt like I knew her."

"Meant to be."

"I guess so."

They ate in silence, and he chuckled as Harmon told him how good everything was after every bite.

"Why do you live in a warehouse? It seems like a lot of space."

"I was homeless for most of my teens. I squatted in an abandoned warehouse in the town where I grew up in Mississippi. It was a poor place, so there wasn't a lot of money to tear down or remodel in the small industrial section. For some reason, I liked the space. The walls never closed in on me. When I moved here, and I saved up enough, I saw this place, and I wanted it. It was in bad shape, but it was better than living in my van or crashing at Lily's place. Some habits don't ever go away."

"I like all the space. My place is tiny. I rent this garage apartment. People ask when I'm going to buy a house or whatever. I just haven't found one to make me want to commit."

"What do you do? I don't think I ever asked."

"Oh, I work at an Atlanta research firm. Mostly, people contact us to investigate art and antiques. Some genealogy projects. Someone always wants to know if they're related to royalty."

"You don't work in town."

"No, most of my time is spent working remotely, but occasionally I stay in Atlanta to take care of anything I can't do from home."

"Wouldn't it be easier to just live there?"

"Probably, but I came here to research family history, and I fell in love with the place. Also, the distance from my family works for me."

"I'm sorry."

"Oh, it's nothing tragic. My parents and sister are very outgoing and athletic. Marathons. Charity events. Very much the life of the rich and famous, or Atlanta royalty. I'm just not very outgoing, and they worry."

"Oh," Harmon uttered that one syllable and then lowered his gaze to the table.

Even as the man tried to hide it, Harmon's insecurity was blatantly on display. For a man as handsome as Harmon was, he didn't think much about himself. That made him sad.

He just softly called Harmon's name and waited for the big man to look at him. The man's beautiful green eyes met his, and he forced a soft smile to ease Harmon's tension.

"Talk to me."

"I like you."

He didn't know how he felt about the misery that stained those three words.

"I like you too. So what's wrong?"

Harmon didn't speak just seemed to choke down the rest of his food, and he did the same. He stood and started to clear the table. He froze with the plates in his hands as Harmon grabbed his hips. He dropped them back onto the table with a clang and let the big man tug him down onto his lap. Harmon's fingertips stroked across his cheek.

"You smell so sweet." Harmon's voice broke.

He closed his eyes as the tip of Harmon's nose moved along

his jaw and down to the side of his neck. A shiver worked through him.

"So soft."

He felt a tug on his bow tie, and then Harmon started to work the buttons of his shirt loose.

"May I just touch you?"

He turned his head, his mouth met Harmon's, and the man's scruff was rough against his smoother skin. He realized with awe that he wasn't the only one shaking. Harmon's breath roughly shuddered over his lips. Harmon held himself so tense that his muscles strained and shook.

"Poe, please."

Something about the begging tone tinged with too much desperation broke him. Harmon shouldn't believe he had to plead for affection or the right to touch. As far as he was concerned, everything he was belonged to Harmon.

"Yes."

Harmon's big hand slipped under the soft linen of his shirt. Harmon squeezed and stroked, pinched his nipples. The man didn't hurry. It was almost as if Harmon savored the moments as if that would be the only time he'd allow Harmon to touch him. He wanted more than a make-out session or some one-night stand. They'd only known each other a few months, but he felt closer to Harmon than he had to anyone else in his life.

Taking chances hadn't always worked in his favor, but he didn't want to bypass the possibility of a relationship with Harmon because he was scared of ruining a friendship. He'd seen the interest and heat in Harmon's eyes as the man studied him. Noticed all the aborted attempts at touching him. Harmon had reached out to him so many times only to stop himself and pull away in every way. The emotional retreat hurt him the most.

"I love touching. Do you want to touch me?"

He frowned at the fearful question. Harmon waited for him to say no and he had no intention of doing that. He stood, and the devastation on Harmon's face broke his heart.

"Take your shirt off, Harmon." Harmon hesitated, and he wasn't having that. "Now."

Harmon's hands trembled as they picked apart the buttons of the wrinkled shirt he wore. He groaned as Harmon exposed his dark skin covered with thick curls. He cataloged scars and a single mole on his right shoulder. The man was physically perfect, and he still didn't understand why Harmon wanted him.

He wasn't going to question it because above everything—including his fear—he wanted to love on this sweet, adorable and insecure man. He didn't close the distance between them until Harmon dropped the shirt to the floor. He moved in close until he pushed his knees against Harmon's and the man parted his legs. He stepped between them.

He let his gaze move over Harmon from his bright jade eyes down to the man's fisted hands on his thick thighs. He raised his right hand and pulled his tie off, and he held it out to Harmon.

"Do you want it?"

Harmon quickly grabbed it and tucked it into the pocket of his jeans. Hiding it as if he'd take it away. He felt powerful and sexy at the heat of Harmon's gaze observing his every movement. The curve of his belly, the slight softness of his chest didn't matter as he removed his shirt. He dropped it. No one had ever looked at him the way Harmon was doing.

He brought his hands to Harmon's scruffy cheeks and bent forward until his mouth touched Harmon's.

Harmon sat stiffly with his hands still clenched on his thighs.

"Don't you want to touch me?"

"Yes."

"Then why aren't you?"

For the first time, he didn't feel insecure about his weight, softness or his thick-framed glasses. Harmon waited for his permission or orders. It was a powerful knowledge.

"I don't want you to go away."

"I'm not going anywhere, baby," he whispered before he took Harmon's lips.

Felt the firm give of Harmon's full lips. He moaned at the strong grip on his hair. Harmon still didn't take over. His cock jerked at Harmon's timidity. He hadn't expected that from Harmon but he should have.

The signs were there all along. His insecurity. The sadness the big man failed to hide. He'd never taken the lead before, and it was oddly exhilarating, but he was slightly lost as well.

Could he take the lead with a man like Harmon? The man was nearly twice his size.

"Do you want me to love on you, baby?" He whispered the question against Harmon's lips.

Harmon nodded in answer causing their mouths to rub together. He straddled the man's lap as he continued to kiss Harmon lazily. Harmon's breath was labored to the point he thought the man would hyperventilate. He softly rubbed his hands over Harmon's chest in a soothing rhythm trying to ease the man's tension.

He tenderly took Harmon's strong jaw in his hands and with feather light touches, he soothed his man. Tried to put Harmon at ease. He tried to ignore the huge hard bulge pushing against his own rigid dick. He didn't see a reason to rush. He wanted to love on Harmon for hours. Show the man how special Poe thought he was.

To him tonight was only the beginning. Unless the man told him, he didn't want anything to do with him he wasn't letting Harmon go. He didn't stop with the kisses. Harmon seemed to move into every brush of his lips. Every nip. The man appeared starved for affection.

How the hell could anyone not want to keep him?

He eased off Harmon's lap, and the almost panicked whimper that passed Harmon's full lips broke his heart.

"It's okay, where's your bedroom?"

"You'll leave me."

Harmon didn't have to explain what that meant. He'd heard enough about no sticking around after a one-night stand. Harmon truly believed that sex would ruin what they had. Yes, he wanted to make love with Harmon. Show the man physically how much he wanted Harmon, but that wasn't what his man needed that night.

"Who says we're going to have sex? This is sort of our official first date. I don't put out on the first date. What if I said I just wanted to spend the night with you? Hold you? Do some making out?"

"Really?"

"Yeah, so, where's your room?"

Harmon stood and carefully laced their fingers. Then the man led him through the dark to metal stairs that led to the second floor. Their steps echoed on the vastness of the space. A dim light shined through the glass of a door you'd see in an office and not a bedroom. Harmon nudged him into a huge room with a big bed in the middle. It was an old-fashioned metal framed bed. A light shone from a bathroom on the other.

He pulled his hand out of Harmon's and backed up until he closed the door. He wanted to see Harmon's reaction. Harmon didn't disappoint, the man's beautiful green eyes watched his every movement. He held his breath as he worked his belt loose, popped the button and eased the zipper down. As he toed his shoes off, he dropped his pants.

No one had ever seen him naked before. Every fuck he'd had was being bent over in the dark. He'd barely enjoyed the times before. He knew he wasn't physically perfect, but the need in Harmon's gaze couldn't be faked. As soon as he was naked, he walked toward the bed. He situated himself with his back against the headboard.

"Undress."

"I thought we weren't…"

"We're not. I just want to feel you while we sleep."

Harmon seemed almost terrified. It was in the way Harmon refused to look at him as he finished undressing and all the while he climbed onto the bed. Harmon stretched out stiffly beside him. He was going to have his work cut out for him.

"Come here," he ordered as he scooted down and waited for Harmon to lay his head on his chest.

Harmon clutched him so tight as if he was frightened that he was going to leave him. He stroked Harmon's soft hair.

He wondered how many people had used and discarded Harmon over the years that the man was so starved for love?

"Are you going to be here in the morning?"

"Yes."

"Okay."

It was too early for him to sleep, but he wanted to hold Harmon. Feel the man close to him and maybe give him some comfort. He liked the man; could see it turning into more. He was fighting against his own insecurities and Harmon's. Nothing made him doubt the way he felt about Harmon, and he'd do whatever he had to, to make sure Harmon always felt special.

He turned his head to brush a kiss to Harmon's brow and smiled as the man snuggled closer. He'd never slept with anyone before, and he closed his eyes to enjoy it. They had a lot to work out, but they had time.

FUCK, NOT NOW!

*T*he beautiful steady thump of a heartbeat under his ear caused him to let out a heavy sigh. His awakening mind let him catalog the other sensations. Smooth, warm skin flush against his bigger and hairier body. The subtle scents of vanilla and ginger, masculine musk, he inhaled it deeply into his lungs. He made himself remember every new sensation and smell. All his defense mechanisms forced him to memorize the details for the lonely days and nights ahead.

The softness and sweetness, Poe was the dream he'd been afraid to remember. Poe, the dangerous rush of a drug through his veins, all the euphoria and pleasure—an overdose of perfection.

He danced his fingertips lightly down the hairless plane of Poe's chest and over the soft curve of his small belly. When he reached the sheet across Poe's hips, he noticed the tight, dark curls and he held his breath as he lifted the covering from Poe's body. He nearly groaned at Poe's thick, pale cock. It was perfect, not too long, but wide enough that his hole clenched at the thought of being filled by it.

He clenched his teeth as he pushed the visions of Poe fucking him away. It would ruin everything. He was broken—something about him made people easily use and discard him. He wanted the small man in his bed to love him—keep him.

Poe's body stretched and arched, a husky moan sounded in the man's throat. "What time is it?"

He dropped the sheet before he got caught looking at Poe. He glanced at the clock on the opposite side of the bed. "Eight."

"Shit, I have to get ready for work."

Poe cursed but didn't jump from the bed, just turned his body and wrapped his hand under his thigh. He gasped as Poe stroked his palm upward to the curve of his ass and he couldn't stop himself from wrapping his right leg around Poe. Their cocks trapped between their bellies. His body and brain warred for control, but the former was winning.

"I could get used to this," Poe groaned.

He tilted his head back as Poe ran his tongue up the front of his throat and then nipped at his chin. He grunted as Poe fisted his left hand in his hair and jerked his head back. Something in the dominant act made him clutch Poe tighter and whimper at the sharp nip of the man's teeth. The fingertips of Poe's right hand played with his hole.

His cock ached and jerked where it lined up with Poe's smaller one.

What happened next shocked him, Poe forcefully slammed his mouth onto his and tongue-fucked him. The push at his hole firmer and he rutted against Poe's stomach. Felt the flesh give and cradle his dick.

"Beautiful how needy you are for me, baby. You want me to fuck you one day?"

He couldn't speak for the pleasure of being in Poe's arms and the man loving on him.

"You want to show me don't you, how gorgeous you are when you break? Show me, now."

Two fingers stretched him wide with a burning pressure—

beautiful pain. He whimpered as he lost control of his body and he rubbed his cock against Poe as the man fucked him so gently with his fingers. He wrapped his arms around Poe's head, their mouths touching as he pushed for release.

"Come on, baby, you know you want to give it to me."

The backs of Poe's fingers tapped his prostate, and he threw his head back. Poe kissed, sucked and bit at his chest.

He was pushed to his back, and he panicked as Poe's touch disappeared, he opened his eyes wide and found Poe crawling between his thighs. Poe didn't break the contact of their eyes as he spat on his fingers and thrust back inside.

"I'll never leave you hanging...never."

He didn't have the time or the ability to respond when Poe swallowed him to the back of his throat. No other experience in his life compared to that one. The slap of Poe's palm against his ass and the suckling sounds of Poe bobbing up and down his cock was almost too much. He wrapped his hands around the back of his thighs and pulled them back to open himself more to Poe.

He felt he should be embarrassed by his high-pitched grunts and the shaking of his body, but he couldn't. He pushed his head into the pillow and lifted his hips higher.

An alarm sounded, shrill and loud letting him know someone was here.

"No," he screamed.

Poe pulled off his cock. "No, you go nowhere until you come. You understand me?"

He nodded as Poe painfully sucked his dick back inside the hot, wet confines of his mouth and doubled the finger pounding of his ass. His short nails dug into his skin, and he let Poe do what he wanted. He felt loved and wanted for the first time in his life.

His toes curled, and every muscle in his body seized as he arched as his release hit him. He shouted as he came and his cock jumped every time he felt Poe swallow. He collapsed, his thighs still spread, and he forced his eyelids up. Poe was smirking as the man crawled to rest between his legs. Poe's lips were tender on his. He darted his tongue out and tasted himself. He shuddered as he felt the thick, fat head of Poe's dick against his hole.

Poe bit his bottom lip and fisted his hand in his hair as the man jerked off.

"I nearly fucking got off just with how you tasted," Poe grunted.

He held Poe's tense body against his and listened to Poe whispering gruffly about what the man loved about him.

"Fuck," Poe yelled through gritted teeth.

Poe's cum spread across his hole and down the crack of his ass. The little man didn't stop until his slight weight relaxed onto his chest. Poe kissed and cuddled him until their breathing returned to normal.

"You better see who that is, I don't think they're going away. I'm going to hop in the shower real quick. Unfortunately, I have to get home. Next time I'll bring my laptop with me, so I don't have to rush."

Poe kissed him once more then crawled off the bed. He couldn't take his gaze off the man until the door closed and blocked his view. He lay there a few more minutes with Poe's cum on him before he made himself get up and pull on a pair of discarded sleep pants from beside his bed.

He should clean up, but he didn't want to wash Poe's scent off him just yet. He needed to savor it a bit longer. He jogged downstairs and toward the doors. He pushed a button on the screen to bring up the camera. He groaned as he noticed a pissed off Linus glaring up at the camera.

"Shit."

He pushed the button to open the doors and waited until Linus stepped inside.

"Took you long enough. Jerk off on your own time." Linus growled and stormed past him.

He rolled his eyes and closed the doors. "I was kinda busy."

"Just because my mother loves your crazy ass doesn't mean I won't fire you."

He resisted the urge to snort. He'd lost count of how many times Linus threatened to lock him up or fire him in the last fifteen years since he'd met the man. If Linus were serious, he would've done it a long time ago.

"Dude, do you ever clean?"

"I kinda got distracted last night. I'll do it later."

Poe and him had left the dinner dishes on the table. He smiled remembering holding the man until he went to sleep and still had Poe tucked against him that morning. He'd never done that before.

"I got a job. It's perfect for you."

Perfect for him, he didn't like the sound of that. The last job that was perfect of him had him acting as a guard for a drug kingpin who was using their client's daughter as a mule. He'd been undercover for three months until the client's daughter showed up. Hunter had hacked into the police database to add a few more pages to his already sketchy record. Said kingpin had several cops on his payroll, and Linus knew the man would run a check.

"I don't want to go undercover."

"Why, you normally eat that shit up, man."

"I just don't—"

"Sorry, I'm not interrupting, am I?" Poe's sweet voice caused him and Linus to turn.

"You leaving?"

"Work calls. But if you don't mind, I'll be back later."

When Poe twined his arms around his neck to pull him down, he didn't fight it. The man didn't censor the possessive kiss.

"You still smell like me. Text me later when you're free."

Poe didn't step away just lowered himself from his toes.

"I'm Solomon Poe," Poe said to Linus and extended his hand.

His boss stared at Poe as if he was waiting to be attacked.

"Linus Trenton."

"I met your mother yesterday. Lovely woman."

"Do you two share meds, Little?"

He was almost offended until Poe laughed. "Be nice to my boyfriend. I have to get going. I'm already late for work."

Poe gave him another quick kiss and hit the remote as he passed the coffee table where the man had left it last night. He pivoted to observe Poe until the doors creaked shut behind him.

"Where the fuck you find him?"

"I kidnapped him."

"I thought Lily was high and imagining things when she told me that story."

He was surprised that Liv hadn't snitched him out to the boss.

"I didn't keep him long," he protested as he walked to the fridge and pulled out one of his coffee energy drinks. He popped the top and turned back to Linus. "So, what's this perfect assignment?"

"A client came to me yesterday."

He took the file Linus handed him. He opened it and scanned the contents.

"His mother married some younger man about a year ago. The client and his mother grew apart over the years, but when he tried to call her for her birthday, the husband said she'd had some kinda breakdown. He had to commit her."

A name caught his attention. "Otto Carrington. I know this guy. He worked at a non-profit clinic in Atlanta. He had a thing for the crazier street kids. One day we'd be meeting up, and they said the doc was going to get them off the streets. Give them free meds and set them up with a new life. I always thought it was bullshit."

"Apparently it is. He still has that clinic, but he's director of a facility in Montgomery, Georgia. Pretty much a no-name town and that Carrington Clinic. Home of the craziest of the rich and famous. He also gets subsidiaries for treating low-income patients, but the very few that have been released had some horror stories to tell."

"But depending on their diagnoses more than likely the doc can spin it into hallucinations."

If people had power and money, they could get away with anything. He'd seen it too many times in his thirty-two years. Especially when he was on the street. The kids got raped and roughed up, cops looked the other way or just took the report and rolled their eyes. He knew there were good cops. Unfortunately, the bad ones got more press.

"Which after Hunter and Peaches did some searching, we think he's using the low-income patients as test subjects. Carrington is also cleared for medical experiments. People swear by their experimental treatments."

"I'm sure the people that can pay their way are getting all the help they need."

"Very true. You know what's weirder?"

He kept scanning the reports. "Dude's first wife killed herself after a stay at Carrington."

"And then Carrington received a very generous donation."

"It seems extreme to drive a wife insane to the point she kills herself or make it appear she killed herself. That's a lot of trouble for an insurance payout."

"It is but a lot safer than getting your hands dirty."

"This has to be more than a job, Linus."

"It is. They're taking advantage of people who don't have anyone to fight for them. I may not know the kids there, but we sure as fuck know ones like them. We're going to take them down."

"When?"

"Strategy meeting Saturday. Is this going to be a problem with the boyfriend? You know we take partner's wishes into account."

"I'll talk to him tonight."

He never had to discuss a job with anyone. Lily and him normally had dinner and a smoke the night before.

"You're going to be on your own once you're inside. You okay with that?"

"As long as they don't go *Manchurian Candidate* on me I think I'll be good."

"We hope it doesn't go that far. Keep the file. Go over it, and we'll put a plan into place."

"Hunter taking care of the backstory for me?"

"We'll have your cover in place by Saturday. Spend a few days with your man, and I'll see you this weekend."

"Good deal."

After he showed Linus to the door and secured his home, he headed to his workstation. Hunter was good, but some things couldn't be hacked.

DID HE CALL HARMON HIS BOYFRIEND?

*W*hat the hell had he done? He panicked through three business calls and one very weird video conference. He'd called Harmon his boyfriend in front of the man's boss. What if—no, Linus was married to two men, Livingston was married to a man, and…shit, he covered his face with his hands. He wasn't cut out for this dominant stuff.

In the moment, he'd felt confident and in control, once he'd made it home all he could think was *what the fuck*. All he'd had to do was picture Harmon all needy and trembling, and his cock instantly hardened. He wanted that again. Him, Solomon Poe, had caused that reaction in a man like Harmon Little. Big and tough, handsome beyond belief, and Harmon was all his.

Nothing changed the fact he wasn't giving Harmon up. If he hadn't believed anything in his almost thirty years on the planet, he was certain the man belonged to him. He checked the time on his laptop and saw it was almost time to clock out for the day. He realized Harmon hadn't texted him.

He closed the lid on his computer and started packing up his work into his messenger bag. He picked up his phone and stroked his thumb across the screen. Instead of sending a message he called Harmon and listened to the rings.

"Shit, I didn't text, I'm so sorry."

"You got busy. It's no big deal. You want company?"

"Yes, you up for a road trip? I gotta check something out in Atlanta and then we can get dinner or whatever."

"If you have to work—"

"I just have to make contact with an acquaintance about a job coming up. We have to talk about that too. How long before you get here?"

"I just packed up some things I need in case I sleep over again."

"You want to stay again?"

The shock was clear in Harmon's question. Did the man actually think that one quickie was enough for him? Not a damn chance. If he'd had his stuff with him, he wouldn't have left Harmon.

"Yes. Do you need anything?"

"No thank you. I'm going to take a shower. I got busy after Linus left and I liked your scent too much."

Harmon's shy tone caused him to smile. He'd never met anyone like Harmon before. What someone saw isn't what they got with the sweet man. He looked big and bad—strong, but inside Harmon was delicate and unsure. How couldn't he not fall for a man like that?

"Get used to it. Go take your shower, and I'll pack an overnight bag."

"Okay. Poe?"

"Yes, baby?"

"I missed you today."

"Me too."

He smiled at Harmon's softly spoken goodbye, and he disconnected the call. After he finished packing up his work, he rushed to his room to throw some clothes and stuff into an old backpack. He made sure to put a few things in that were Harmon's favorite color.

A chuckle slipped out as he remembered the way Harmon had snatched his bow tie and tucked it into his pocket. That was two Harmon was in possession of, and he doubted they'd be the last. No one had ever been turned on by his nerdy bow tie fetish. He grabbed his bags and made his way to the door turning off everything as he went.

His apartment was the size of Harmon's bedroom. It worked well for him, and one day he'd find a house he wanted to buy.

His parents and sister loved him. They just didn't always get him. They wanted him happy. He wondered what they'd think of Harmon. They'd be shocked if he ever brought anyone home. He'd come out with no scandal. His parents waved it off as if he was announcing the weather. His sister smiled and tried to start hooking him up with some of her friends.

The guys he'd dated never felt right, and he and Harmon hadn't met under normal circumstances. He laughed at the thought of telling his family how he'd met Harmon.

He relaxed on the half hour drive to Harmon's place. He pulled to a stop beside Harmon's motorcycle. The man waved as he turned off the engine and exited.

"We taking that?"

"You've ridden before."

"Once, with Livingston and that man has no sense of obeying the speed limit."

"Liv isn't much on rules."

He rolled his eyes as he shook his head and stepped up to Harmon. He slipped his arms around the man's waist and lifted onto his toes. As soon as their mouths met, he raised his left hand to curve around the back of Harmon's head. His tongue stroked along the subtle part of the man's lips, and when Harmon moaned, he pushed inside. The kiss intensified from gentle to rough in seconds. Their breathing turned harsh as they ate at each other's mouths. He couldn't get Harmon close enough.

His hands ached to stroke over Harmon's hairy skin. He wanted to palm the man's hips as he bent Harmon over the seat of the bike. Being a slave to his emotions—his lust—was an odd sensation. He'd never craved someone as much as he did Harmon. To him the man was irresistible.

Fuck it, he jerked away and kept his focus on Harmon's dazed expression and quickly popped the button on his jeans and slowly drew the zipper down. He dropped to his knees and tugged Harmon's pants down to mid-thigh.

Harmon's veiny dick was hard, and the head was wet. He swiped his tongue over the slit as he wrapped his hand firmly around the base. He gently sucked on the tip and savored the masculine musk of Harmon's precum.

He didn't care they were out in the open, and anyone could pull up. The only thing he wanted was Harmon fucking his mouth and letting him swallow every drop. Harmon placed his hands on either side of his head and began a slow thrust and retreat. He relaxed his throat so Harmon could bottom out.

He squeezed Harmon's fuzzy ass cheeks and dug his fingertips into the man's crease. He fingered the tight, wrinkled hole and that was all it took. Harmon lost control. Fucking his mouth in a brutal rhythm as the tips of his middle fingers breached Harmon's body. He sucked hard as Harmon tried to pull out.

His man whimpered his name. Begged and pleaded, he loved the sexy high-pitched whine. He'd never topped before but he wanted it, and he needed it now. He slowly bobbed along Harmon's dick a few more times before he released him and surged to his feet.

"Tell me you have condoms and lube." He demanded against Harmon's lips.

"Y-yes. In my room. Nightstand."

He didn't wait, he grabbed Harmon's hand and dragged him

into the warehouse. He practically ran up the steps. Harmon's jeans were still trapped around his thick furry thighs.

"Bend over the bed."

Harmon looked scared and more than a little nervous. He didn't want the man to have time to think.

"Don't make me say it again, Harmon."

He didn't know where the steel-edged tone came from, but it came too easily. Harmon bent over and placed his hands on the unmade bed.

He could barely take his gaze off the flexed muscled cheeks as he searched through the drawer for a condom and lube. He tossed the items on the mattress and stepped up behind Harmon. He pushed his hand between Harmon's thighs and gave his cock a few rough strokes. As Harmon was distracted, he brought his right hand down on one cheek then the other, repeatedly until Harmon lifted on the toes of his boots. Harmon's back bowed pushing his ass higher.

"I want you naked. Stand up and turn around."

Harmon did as he ordered him. He gazed up at Harmon and reached for the hem of the man's black t-shirt. He eased it up the sexy hairy belly, exposed Harmon's powerful chest, and the big man lifted his arms to allow him to remove the shirt.

"I can't believe you want me."

"How could you not believe it?" he asked. "You're sweet, sexy, and adorable." He moved closer and pressed a kiss to the center of Harmon's chest. "I can't believe no one has ever wanted to keep you, but you're mine." He nipped at Harmon's skin and smirked at the man's deep groan. "I have no intention of letting you go."

He dropped to his knees and unzipped Harmon's boots, removed them slowly as he felt the man watching him.

"Please, don't say something you don't mean. I—"

"I'll never say anything I don't mean."

He stripped his man of the rest of his clothes, then socks until Harmon stood perfectly naked.

"Do you want me to love on you, baby?"

He didn't remember a time someone turned him on as much as Harmon. The surprising sweetness and insecurity of his man so at odds with the strong, fearless man. Harmon trembled and his pale eyes filled with tears.

"Oh, baby, don't do that." He quickly got to his feet and took Harmon's face in his hands.

He pulled Harmon down as he kissed the saltiness of tears from Harmon's thick lashes.

"I've thought about you all day. The way you felt against me as you slept. I couldn't take my eyes off you."

He took a few steps backward. Toed off his shoes, removed his clothes until he was as naked as Harmon.

"You like what you see, Harmon?"

His confidence flared back to life at Harmon's rapt attention. It was a novel experience to elicit that response from a man especially one like Harmon. He brought his hand to his dick and stroked along the thick width.

"Talk. Use your words, baby."

"You're so fucking beautiful."

Harmon wasn't just saying the words—the man actually believed him beautiful.

"And what am I, Harmon?"

"Mine?"

"No question about that. Lie down for me."

Harmon, like last night, stretched out stiffly on the bed and scooted to the center. "Do you want me to turn over?"

"No, baby, I want to see those pretty eyes while I make you mine."

He crawled onto the bed and between Harmon's spread legs. He sat back on his heels. His hands shook slightly as he opened the condom and rolled it on.

"You're shaking, baby."

"I'm nervous."

"Why are you nervous?"

"I said I wouldn't bottom again until it meant something."

"I don't mind if you want to—"

"No, please, I want you inside me."

"Well, we're both nervous then because I've never topped before." He spoke as he opened the bottle and added slick to his fingers.

Harmon grabbed the back of his thighs and pulled them back. He groaned at how sexy his man was all open and vulnerable. As he blanketed Harmon's body with his, he teased the man's tight hole. He kissed his man. Loved him all gentle and slow as he worked one finger in and out, added a second and third. Their sweaty bodies slid easily together as he got his gorgeous man ready. He lifted up enough to study Harmon's flushed face and the way Harmon had his eyes squeezed shut as the man fucked himself on his fingers.

He removed his fingers from Harmon and added lube to his latex covered cock. He cleaned his hand on the sheet and took his dick and lined it up with Harmon's stretched hole. Nudging his hips forward, he threw his head back as the tightest pressure engulfed him.

He thrust forward in a slow, gentle glide until he was balls deep.

He lowered his mouth to Harmon's and kissed his man as he fucked Harmon tenderly. Harmon's heels pushed into his ass cheeks, and they moved in a sensuous rhythm. He tasted the salt of tears and sweat as his man cried, whispered nonsense words.

Holding Harmon. Loving on him. This wasn't about fucking. He needed their first time to prove to Harmon that all he wanted was to love on him—keep him for more than one night.

"You're so perfect. Fuck, baby, made for me."

Their pace increased, and he shifted his hips until he heard

Harmon gasp. Harmon froze and trembled. He pushed upward, wrapped his hands over the front of Harmon's thighs and pulled him onto his dick.

"Look at how pretty you look on my dick."

Harmon lifted onto his elbows and looked at where they were connected.

Harmon was stretched so tight around his cock that the rim flexed as he pushed inside and the drag of Harmon's muscles and hole was almost more than he could take. Sweat poured down his temples, chest and the indent of his spine. Pleasure burned through him and tensed his muscles.

He loved everything about Harmon from his darkly flushed skin to the coarse, thick hair that covered his groin and ass. Harmon fell back onto the bed and curled his hands around the metal bars of the headboard. The big man's body twisted and shuddered.

"Fuck me, please," Harmon begged.

He didn't hesitate. He took Harmon's angrily flushed cock into his hand and fucked his man just like he wanted. Skin slapped against skin. He matched each thrust to the pace he jacked his man's dick. For the first time in his life, he lost control. The more Harmon screamed and grunted the harder he fucked his man. Every muscle in his body screamed for release, and as he gritted his teeth, Harmon shouted and painted his belly with cum. The vise-like grip had him slamming forward once more, and he fell onto Harmon. Took his baby's mouth in a hard kiss as Harmon's arms circled him, he rode out his release in small, shallow thrusts.

Their harsh breathing, the squeak of the bed, and their quiet groans were the only sounds that filled the room.

"Did you say something about going somewhere?" His words muffled against Harmon's throat. He sucked lightly at the jump of Harmon's pulse.

"Did I? I don't remember."

He chuckled as he lifted enough to reach between them and held onto the condom as he eased from Harmon.

"I feel so empty."

"We'll be doing this a lot, I promise. I'm going to get cleaned up, want to join me?"

He took Harmon's hand as he knee-walked off the bed and tugged until Harmon was off the bed. He couldn't resist one more kiss. Then he led his man to the bathroom. Harmon seemed almost shy. He'd have to work on that. He didn't want his man to doubt what was between them. Falling for Harmon was so easy—the easiest thing he'd ever done.

HARMON WANTED TO GO HOME AND
HAVE HIS MAN LOVE ON HIM

*H*e had Poe tucked against his chest as he let his gaze move around the bar. With years of practice, he noticed the exchange of cash for baggies. Talent in the back lining up a trick for an hour or two. He wanted to go home and curl up with his man. Poe didn't belong in a place like that. He didn't belong with him at all.

Poe had given him everything he'd ever wanted in a lover. Gentle and passionate, showed him what it was like to be needed. He could still feel the way Poe had loved him. Kissed him at the end, then took him to the shower and washed him. The touches hadn't stopped. Poe had held tight to his waist on the trip to Atlanta. Laced their fingers when they walked into the bar. Poe hadn't left him since.

As was his habit, his brain tried to calculate how long he had with Poe. He lowered his head to nuzzle Poe's cheek with his and caught movement at the door. The first thing he noticed was hot pink hair. Trevor hadn't changed much since the last time he'd seen him. Ex-street kid. Married, but he wasn't a fan of the kid's husband. The older man put him on edge.

Fucking finally! He spun to put his back to the room and

braced himself with one hand on the wall above Poe's head. He might act like he was crazy and was able to pull it off well, but he was also damn good at his job. It was the one thing he'd always taken pride in.

"The cutie with the pink hair the one you've been waiting for?"

"How did you notice that?"

"You were rubbing up on my back before he walked in. I took a guess. Should I be jealous?"

He started to laugh until he noticed a hardness to Poe's gaze. Shit, his man was jealous.

"Now, Poe, why would I look at anyone else when I've got you?"

The cute blush on his man's face caused him to smile but the fact the man cared made him awestruck. His man was beautiful and smart, sexy and, fuck, the list could go on.

Trevor came up beside them and spun until his back was to the wall. "I hope I'm not interrupting."

"Hi, Trevor, this is my man, Poe, Poe, meet Trevor."

"Finally, someone got smart and snatched your ass up. Sexy man like you being single…tragic. So, what did I do to earn a visit from *the* Harmon Little himself?"

"I need some info, and you haven't been off the streets long enough to be out of the loop."

"Shame, you're only after my mind."

He snorted as Trevor winked at him and Poe's hands fisted in his t-shirt. "You might want to knock down the flirting. I don't think my man likes it."

"Possessive, I can so understand that. Buy me food."

Trevor pushed off the wall and retraced his steps. He took Poe's hand and followed. Trevor was obsessed with his stomach. Too many years of going hungry. Trevor had been a chunky thirteen-year-old when he'd met him. That was five years ago, and the kid hadn't changed much. Even all the shit the kid had gone through Trevor hadn't lost his innocence or his positive attitude. Even on the small side, the kids looked up to Trevor—knew the kid was the one to come to when someone needed to hide for a while.

"Interesting kid."

He glanced down at Poe as they stepped out onto the sidewalk. He shook his head as he watched Trevor hand out condoms and cards with a list of shelters and clinics.

"He's been out here a long time."

Trevor stopped outside a rundown diner.

"How did you meet him?"

Trevor answered, "I tried to fuck him."

"You didn't try too hard."

"I was thirteen and hungry, your van looked warm, and you smelled of weed, so I didn't think I had to worry about you being a cop." Trevor flipped him off and pulled open the diner door.

"Are all your friends weird?"

"No, well, yeah, okay, they're all weird in some way. I like being the normal one."

Poe stopped, pivoted on his toes and tilted his head all the way back. He glared as the man rolled his lips between his teeth, but that didn't hide the tilted corners of Poe's mouth.

"I don't like you."

Poe's mouth pulled into a wide grin and the man raised onto his toes. "Aw, Harmon, you know you love me."

The kiss was too quick, but Poe pulled away before he had a chance to bring him flush and deepen the caress.

Goddammit, he cursed as Poe left him on the sidewalk. Before he had time to panic he went to join Poe and Trevor, they were already looking over menus and talking quietly. He approached the table.

"I ordered you an apple juice. They don't serve energy drinks."

They ordered enough food for twenty people, and Trevor sipped his drink until the waitress disappeared.

"So, what do you need?"

"Carrington."

"The doc with a Messiah Complex, but that's typical of mega-lomaniacs with type A personalities. What's he done now?"

"Done now?"

"Dude, some of the kids have been showing up lately damn near catatonic. No one knows shit and getting information out of them is impossible. They're so fucking fried I don't think they know their own names. Sonja showed up a few months ago. Pupils so blown I took her to the ER to see if she'd OD'd. The drug test came back negative, but she was on something."

"If you had to guess?"

"Antipsychotics, I don't know, a lot of the kids I keep an eye on have mental health or addiction problems. I've seen the effect of just about every med out there. Whatever it was, it was strong as fuck. People swear every day by experimental treatments. They just want to be normal and some of the kids...they want something different. I didn't want to sell my ass or give old dude's blowjobs to survive, but we do what we gotta do."

He'd told Trevor plenty of times he had nothing to be ashamed of, but he knew it didn't help. Looking back on his past, he knew some of that shit still shaped who he was. No amount of forgiveness could wash it all away.

Poe must have sensed his unease and leaned into his side, rubbed his thigh in a soothing motion.

"You did good for yourself, Little. How did you snag the cutie?"

"He kidnapped me."

"Oh fuck, I gotta hear this one."

"You started it." He turned to smile up at the waitress as she arrived at the table with an overflowing tray.

Once they were situated with their orders and drinks were refilled, Poe started their story.

"I was in a grocery store aisle looking at weight loss—"

He growled at the thought his man needed to lose a pound. If people were happy why did everyone expect them to change? He loved Poe's softness—the way the man felt in his arms.

"As I was saying, I was starving, exhausted and sore from the sadist known as my personal trainer. All of sudden I'm knocked to the ground. This strange guy says come with me and the next thing I know I'm in his van. Come to find out he kidnapped me because his best friend said when he found his person it would feel like lightning struck."

Trevor sighed. "That's so romantic."

"I swear, Harmon, your friends are weird."

"Like I said, I like being the normal one."

Trevor choked as the man laughed and he felt no pity. Trevor cleared his throat. "Little was a fixer on the streets. We had issues we always came to him. We knew he was working free-lance for the cops and a few other things, but Little was the man to trust. He was like us. Been there. Done that. Nothing's changed."

He ignored the compliments and focused on his food. He didn't think he'd done all that much. When he was out in the cold, he'd wished for someone to have his back. Someone to be there when he didn't have a place to run. He didn't spend much time there anymore, but all the kids knew they could call him anytime with no questions asked. It wasn't much, but it turned out to be something he could do.

"You going after Carrington?"

"A job came my boss' way, and he needed someone who can blend. If it turns out he's using street kids to test his so-called miracle drugs we need to take him down."

"Big name, man, he's on speed dial for every cop who comes across a tweaked-out kid. Heard a few rumors cops make commissions."

"Wouldn't be surprised. Won't be the first time I went toe-to-toe with the police."

"Yeah, man, but this is different. There's a lot of money floating around."

"You're not telling me something."

"It's just rumors, nothing concrete. You know how people like to talk."

"Doesn't mean it ain't true."

"Carrington likes to play with the kids. Doesn't like them too young, but he's offering them salvation and some of us will pay whatever price. Heard he gets a bit rough. Can't bring you anyone who can corroborate, though."

"So, not only is he performing experiments, he's molesting them as well." Poe's voice was soft.

He glanced to find his man pissed off.

"Not much recourse for us out there. Some of us are lucky to get off the streets. Find a nice steady job. Get set up in a long-term shelter that'll help us with housing, but the ones that are fucked-up they take the scraps."

He understood that. He'd been one of the kids that took the scraps. He had a job and a home, didn't put out for a wad of cash, but he'd exchanged the monetary benefits for the illusion of affection. Broken people would do anything for love—a moment of belonging—to forget that they lived a nightmare. He feared his voice would break, so he didn't respond.

"I won't pretend to understand. My family is loving. They didn't bat an eye when I came out. What that doctor is doing needs to stop."

"It does, but in the wrongness of it, there's option. Even if the option is false we can pretend for a minute it's real. It's a hot meal. A warm bed. Medicine to make all the mental bullshit go away. One kid didn't know what was real or imagined. He just wanted the voices to stop telling him to harm others and himself. To be promised that it'll all go away, wouldn't you jump at that chance?"

They lapsed into silence as they finished eating, and he didn't miss that Trevor kept glancing at his phone. The man's soft, innocent face pulled tighter into a grimace.

"I can take care of it."

"I made my choice, Little."

"Doesn't mean you can't change your mind."

"You'll be the first one I call."

"Fair enough."

He didn't feel right leaving at that, but he couldn't force Trevor to accept his help. Not every decision in life could be categorized into black and white columns—right or wrong. Life wasn't so concrete or easy. He asked some more questions, and Trevor hung out for another hour before the kid made his excuses. He forced himself to relax until Trevor was gone.

"So, you got a bad feeling?"

How could Poe pick up on his emotions so easily after only months of being friends?

"About a year ago, I was out here hanging with some of the kids. Checking in. Dropping off some supplies. Condoms. Lube. Shuttling some to the clinic. If I'm not here to do it, Trevor reminds them to get tested at least every six months. Trevor had a regular. Seemed like a decent guy. Trevor said the guy just wanted his company more than he wanted the sex. I don't have an issue with age differences. Bull and Gregory, Livingston and Fielding. I don't see a problem, but this guy seemed too nice."

"How can someone be too nice?"

"You're paying someone to fuck. Essentially, you're a product, and some of the clients treat you like one too. Something disposable. There's nothing wrong with sex work, and not everyone's experience is bad. Although, too many times on the street it can go to shit."

"Yeah, some people like the companionship. If you're lucky, you get dinner and conversation before they demand the sex."

"Harmon, is that—"

"Can we talk about it somewhere else?"

In his gut, he knew the conversation would have to happen at some point. Part of him hoped that it never did, but honesty was a big thing. Lily always told him she and Damon would never have worked without it. He paid the ticket and took Poe's hand.

He had parked his bike at the office Linus kept in the city. They had a bit of a walk.

"If you don't want to talk about it. I don't need to know."

"My mother surrendered her rights when I was five, maybe six. I don't remember much. All I do remember is going from a crowded group home to a series of foster homes. They said I had an unnatural attachment. Fuck, all I could remember was I loved hugs and affection. I just wanted to be near someone." He refused to look at Poe. Just held the man's smaller hand as they walked along like they were a normal couple. Poe had gotten a bad deal when the man got stuck with him.

"Come on, keep going."

"When I found out the last foster family I was with was sending me back because it seemed I wasn't a good fit, I ran. It was a small city. Poor as fuck. I was thirteen when I started living on the streets. Sometimes I'd get picked up and taken back, but mainly I learned how to hide. Something else I learned, sex made me forget. It wasn't the type of affection I wanted, but it served a purpose."

"Touch and companionship?"

"I was wanted. Men, women, men liked to fuck me and women wanted to be fucked by me. I was big for my age. Tall and muscular enough they all thought I was at least seventeen. If you don't want to, ya know, be with me because of what I did, I won't blame you."

"Shut up, Harmon, you survived, and if you hadn't, I wouldn't have been snatched by you, and that's one thing I won't regret. Besides, I'm looking forward to telling my parents and sister how we met."

"Don't do that."

"Already in the plan." Poe paused and pulled him to a stop. "Harmon, you may be a tad crazy and more than a little bit of a slob, but what this is between us I won't ever regret it. You like me as I am and I'll respect you in the same way. You are who you are, Harmon, the bad and the good made you"—Poe poked his chest—"who you are. I wish you hadn't gone through what you did. But I won't shame you for it. It's in the past."

"Not the distant past, though. You remember Fielding's stalker?"

"Yeah."

"The guy came up to me in a bar. I fucked him because I was flattered and jealous. I knew nothing more than he was some guy at Brawlers, but he saw me as a weak link…his way in."

"Again, not going to shame you. People have one-night stands. Sexual partners they'll never see again. What someone does with their own body isn't my business. I do blame the men and women who did take advantage of teenage you. I've had a few temporary partners. Blind dates that turned into one night of fucking. I'd be a hypocrite if I made you feel bad for getting off."

"You're too good to me."

"Harmon, my sweet crazy man, I'll always be good to you."

"I should've taken you somewhere more romantic. Candle-light and all that."

"I'm not really the candlelight and all that sort of person. Heavy subjects but I enjoyed dinner with you and a friend of yours."

"You're too nice."

"No, I'm not and just to prove it, we're going to my parents' place."

"They'll be asleep, it's late."

"Nope, not asleep, they're about ready to come home from a charity event. We're crashing in the guest house."

"Charity event. Guesthouse. That is so not my scene."

"Too damn bad. I texted my mom while you got ready earlier and told her I was bringing my boyfriend by."

"Why would you do that?"

"Harmon Little, you're meeting my parents. Get over it. Now, let me tell you what I plan to do when I have you all to myself later."

He groaned as his cock hardened as Poe whispered about all the things the small man wanted to do to him. He didn't know how he made it back to the garage to get his bike. It took the edge off his nervousness but didn't in anyway alleviate it completely. Poe wanted him to meet the parents. He'd never met parents before, hell, he'd never had a partner before. This was a nightmare scenario. What if Poe's family didn't like him? Would Poe break up with him for someone more appropriate?

This was a fucking nightmare.

POE'S MAN WAS GOING TO PUKE

*H*is first true attempt at being an understanding boyfriend or partner or whatever the hell he turned into was an epic failure. Harmon, his poor man, was completely losing his shit. He was an asshole for finding that comical and that was never part of his personality until he met Harmon. Harmon sweated profusely. If he wasn't mistaken, the man was on the border of a full-blown panic attack.

He rubbed Harmon's lower back in a soothing rhythm as he opened the front door. He nudged Harmon inside and kicked the door shut.

"Anybody home," he called out.

"Solomon, you finally got here."

Salome Poe glided into the room in a beautiful silver evening gown. He rushed toward his mother as he smiled at her. He hugged her tight around her slender waist as she squeezed him tight, rocking him back and forth.

"Mom, you're looking gorgeous as always."

He stepped back and took her hands to hold her arms out to the side. He noticed his dad stood in the doorway of the sitting room. Six-feet-three inches of imposing man in a tuxedo. He resisted the urge to shake his head as he compared himself to his parents and his sister who thankfully wasn't there. Harmon wouldn't survive a meeting with his sister, Sandra, yet.

"Flattery won't get you out of being fussed at for six months of no visits."

"I know, I'm a horrible son. How haven't you disowned me yet?"

"You're less of a pain in the ass than your sister."

He and his sister were almost eight years apart in age. He'd done his best at the annoying baby brother act, and she'd threatened to kill him thousands of times. Sandra had their parents to herself for a long time, and she hadn't hidden her dismay at having to share them with an annoying sibling. Even worse that it was a brother. They'd grown closer when he'd hit his teens, and she'd been off to college. Then when he'd come out, she'd been all about setting him up on dates.

"I'm so snitching you out."

"Introduce me to your gentleman." Salome moved to his side and slid her arm around his.

He led her to where Harmon stood. The big man had his hands shoved into his pockets and focused on the toes of his scuffed boots.

"Mom, this is Harmon Little, Harmon?" Harmon didn't look up. "Harmon." He raised his hand to press his fingertips under Harmon's scruffy chin and lifted his gaze. He smiled reassuringly at Harmon. "Harmon, this is my mom, Salome."

"Pretty name."

"Thank you, Harmon. Honey, you don't have to be nervous."

He'd worship his mother forever as she instantly moved away from him and enveloped Harmon. His mom was a few inches shorter than Harmon at almost six-foot.

"I was so happy when Solomon called to say he was bringing his boyfriend home. Come on and meet my husband."

He retreated to let his mom take over. If Harmon saw his

parents were normal people, no matter the trappings, he hoped Harmon would relax.

"Kyler, this is Harmon."

"How ya doing, son, nice to meet ya." His dad's thick Texan accent made him remember the story of how his parents met. Salome had fallen in lust with a twenty-year-old ranch hand who worked for her college best friend's father. She'd sworn the man was going to be hers no matter what she had to do.

His dad held out his hand and thankfully didn't react when it took Harmon a minute to respond.

"Nice to meet you, sir."

"No sir around here, Harmon, want a drink?"

"I don't drink."

"I think we have some sodas or Solomon told me you liked apple juice. I picked some up earlier."

"That would be great."

"Well, you gentlemen go have a seat, and I'll get you your juice."

"I don't want to be trouble."

"It's a walk to the kitchen, Harmon."

He retook possession of his boyfriend as his mom disappeared then they followed his dad into the sitting room. He pushed Harmon down on one of the sofas. Shortly, everyone was set up with drinks and Harmon seemed to be braced for the worst.

"What is it you do, Harmon?" his dad asked.

Salome was sitting beside her husband and curled against his side. His parents didn't care if they were in public or alone, they never tempered their love for each other. He'd always wanted a relationship like theirs.

"I work for a company called Trenton Security. We specialize in bodyguard services, and we freelance for a bail bondman's business as Bail Enforcement Agents. I mostly work as a surveillance expert."

"Sounds like an exciting but dangerous life."

When his dad tensed, it was obvious just the thought of him being involved with someone with a dangerous job bothered him. They might talk to him alone later to make sure he was sure of his decision. Nothing would make him leave Harmon. He'd waited too long for a man of his own.

"It has its moments, but I'm good at it. Me and my teammates are more like family than co-workers."

"Is that something you've always done, Harmon?" His mom must have noticed her husband's discomfort because she rubbed his chest as she took over the conversation.

"I started working in security when I was eighteen. I have a talent for getting in and out of places without being seen. So my current boss set me up testing security systems."

"Everyone should do something they enjoy with their life. It's too short to be miserable. Solomon didn't tell us how the two of you met."

He couldn't contain his laughter at the panic on Harmon's face at Salome's interest.

"Um, I ran into him in a grocery store."

"He had the uncontrollable urge to take me home with him."

"Solomon."

"Mom, it was completely innocent. He finds me irresistible in my bow ties."

He relaxed some when Harmon seemed to do the same when he didn't bring up the kidnapping.

"Glad you finally found someone who appreciates your quirks." His mom seemed so serene as she talked.

His parents were the coolest people he knew. They both came from money but never let that shape them. Kyler had taken a few years off after high school for work on a ranch. Salome went straight to college to become a doctor when her parents wanted her to marry and be the dutiful wife. He loved that they went against expectations. He was also a little jealous of their fearlessness. That was one of the reasons he loved Harmon. Harmon had his issues. Yet the man knew who he was, faults and all, and accepted them.

"He's beautiful."

Harmon said it so quietly he almost missed it, but he looked up to find Harmon watching him with that adoring expression he'd come to crave. He turned his head and rested his cheek against Harmon's thick bicep to find his parents watching them with small smiles.

"He is. I can tell my son is happier and more comfortable in his skin since the last time we saw him. He's always been a bit insecure. Kyler and I have tried to make him more confident, but we weren't successful."

"He's smart, gorgeous, funny, cute..." Harmon's voice trailed off. "He was looking at diet sh...stuff when we met."

"Solomon Arthur Poe, what have we discussed?"

"Mom, I wasn't taking diet pills. I was looking at protein bars and—"

"Don't try that bullshit with your mother, son. You're healthy, and you eat right, unless you want to lose weight, you shouldn't torture yourself. We didn't raise you and your sister to be self-conscious."

He lowered his head at his dad's mini-speech. They never made him feel bad about being chunky. Only that didn't mean he hadn't let society get him down. Everyone had something they didn't like about themselves. It was a natural human reaction.

"Sorry, and you don't have to look smug, Little." He elbowed Harmon in the ribs.

"I don't like when you call me Little."

"I'm sorry, baby." He soothed his man.

Harmon seemed to take small things personally. Like him using his last name like everyone else had done. Or things he didn't even notice until he picked up on Harmon's insecurity. It wasn't an overblown reaction. Harmon had some deep-rooted scars the man hid beneath humor and crazy behavior. Unless it affected their relationship in an adverse way, he had no intention of changing his man. If Harmon needed to be comforted, then that's what he would do.

"Do you have any family, Harmon?"

"No biological family. My mother gave me up when I was a kid. I have my friends and their husbands and wives, partners. I have a lot of nieces and nephews. My best friend, Lily, and her husband are like a mom and dad."

"Well, you can consider us family now too. We always wanted more kids after Solomon, but we just weren't lucky enough. Maybe one day our children will give us some grandchildren to spoil."

"Mom, we've talked about this."

"You want kids?"

He turned his attention back to Harmon. "I never really thought about it. I don't see myself as a parent."

"Me neither. I like being an Uncle. My life isn't suitable for mini-humans. What if one day I don't come home from a job?"

That eased his tenseness some. It wasn't that he didn't like kids or whatever, he just couldn't see himself at this point in his life being responsible enough for kids. He'd couldn't even commit to having a pet. The last plant he had, he'd killed it when he forgot to water it.

He didn't like thinking that Harmon wouldn't come home one night, but he couldn't say he hadn't thought about Harmon's job. He'd heard the stories the times he'd hung out with Fielding and Livingston. It wasn't enough to make him step back. One more day was better than missing out on a single minute of being with Harmon.

"Have you ever been hurt at work?"

"No, we have vests, and we watch each other's backs. Not saying we haven't had to take cover. We know our job."

The conversation went to lighter subjects until his mom

started to nod off where her head rested on his dad's shoulder.

"I think it's time to take my beautiful wife to bed. She got your room ready earlier. Keep it down...there's some things a parent doesn't need to hear."

His dad winked, and he laughed as his parents said goodnight. He didn't take his gaze off them until they exited the room.

"That wasn't too bad, was it?"

"I expected something different."

"I know you thought they'd be snobby because of the money and all that, but I know them. They're great and don't care much for expectations or what they're supposed to do. Even if they were the way you assumed they would be, it wouldn't change the way I feel about you. Okay?"

"Okay."

He crossed his left arm over his chest and placed it on Harmon's right cheek to turn his head until he could place his mouth on Harmon's. Each kiss felt more amazing than the one before. He loved the freedom to touch Harmon. To show the man exactly how he felt. He wasn't ready to confess his feelings. Harmon was still skittish and questioning. It hurt a bit, but since he knew Harmon's past, he tried not to let it bother him. All he could do was prove to Harmon he was in it for the long haul. If it took days or years, he'd make sure Harmon never doubted the man was his and he belonged to Harmon heart and soul.

"Come on, bedtime. We have to get up early to head home."

"Linus gave me some days off before we meet up Saturday to spend time with you."

"Maybe I'll call in and take a few days. I haven't taken time off since last year. Would you like that? Just the two of us at your place?"

"I'd really like that."

"Let's get ready for bed, and I'll call and leave a message for my boss."

He stood and took Harmon's hand. He slowly led Harmon up

to his room. He couldn't believe a few months ago he was killing himself to be something he wasn't in order to get a man. Being who he was turned out to be enough for the right man. Who the hell would've thought that it took getting snatched from a grocery store diet aisle to find his happy ever after?

* * *

THEY STOOD OUTSIDE beside the front entrance of *Vincent's,* and he was about to smack Harmon's hands away from the tie. Harmon had come down from the bedroom appearing uncomfortable in the button-down shirt, tie and dress pants. He'd kept telling Harmon they could stay in, but the next day Harmon was supposed to be leaving for a job.

The man hadn't gone into details and part of him, while curious, didn't really want to know. Especially if the assignment turned out to be dangerous.

"Harmon, we can go home." Harmon's comfort had become his top priority. His man's life hadn't been the easiest, and he needed to change that.

They'd talked about their pasts, and Harmon deserved to be treated gently, with respect and love.

"No, I want to take you on a romantic date. Do the grown up thing."

"You know I like staying in. Means I get to curl up on the couch and touch you whenever I want." He stepped up beside Harmon and slipped his arms around the man's waist. He tipped his head back to smile up at Harmon. They'd been dancing around the dating thing for months. Yet even as they pretended to be friends, they'd still dated in their own way.

Maybe in some ways, he'd fallen too hard and fast. He knew others would find it weird how him and Harmon came to be, but to him it was right. He wanted his man to be comfortable, and this didn't seem like Harmon's kind of place.

"You do that anyway."

The corners of his mouth tugged into a grin, and he rose onto his toes. He brought his hand up to Harmon's cheek and pressed his mouth to Harmon's. He brushed a kiss to the firm curves. "Yeah, I love touching you."

"So, let me do this. I leave tomorrow, and I told you I'd try to call, but it might not happen. I don't like it. I shouldn't have agreed."

"Baby, you love your job. I'll be nervous while you're gone, but I know you'll be fine."

"Come on, I called Vincent earlier and reserved a table."

"You know as long as I've lived here this will be the first time I've come here."

"Vincent's is mainly for partners who want to something romantic."

"Then I can't wait." As he spoke, he stepped away and took Harmon's hand, lacing their fingers and led the man inside.

Tables for two and some larger littered the room. They were covered with linen cloths and electric candles.

"Uncle Little!"

A pretty, teenage girl in a flowing linen sheath dress that conformed to full curves approached them. Bright thread wraps were streaked through her curly dark hair that was twisted into an elegant yet loose bun. He couldn't contain his laughter as he found Harmon being squeezed within an inch of his life. A flash of recognition teased at the back of his mind and realized he'd seen a picture of her. He couldn't remember her name, though.

"Princess, as beautiful as always." Harmon extricated himself from the bear hug and lovingly gazed at the girl as he held her arms out to the side.

"Aw, thanks, Uncle Little. Lucky just made it for me. So..." A wicked grin transformed the rounded features. "Gonna introduce me to the hottie?"

"He's mine."

"You know, he's pretty, but he's not my type."

"Still dating that biker chick you met at your last tattoo convention?"

Princess rolled her beautiful blue eyes in that professional level all teenage girls had.

"Too much distance and you know Juvie is a full-time job. She hates sharing me."

Juvie, he recognized that name, she was the daughter of Little's friend, Scary, and the man's two husbands. He spent a lot of nights laughing his ass off at Little's stories of what the Crews called the Hellions. They seemed a handful but extremely loved even with their many quirks.

"That best friend of yours—"

The young lady shoved Little's chest. "Don't start. I love her, you know that."

"Yeah, and when are you going to do something about that?"

"Can I show you to your table?"

"Smooth subject change."

"Yeah, yeah."

"Princess, this is my Poe. Poe, this is the beautiful, Mina *Princess* Carver. She belongs to Trouble and Brody."

"I know Brody from the grocery store. It's pleasure to meet you, Princess."

"You too, Poe. It's taken Little long enough to find himself a person. Come on, I'll show y'all to your table."

Apparently, Princess was finished with any conversation about her crush on her best friend. She led them to a round table in the back, and Harmon pulled out his chair, then pushed it in as he sat down. Princess told them the specials, took their drink order, and left them with menus. She said their server would be right with them.

He glanced around, "This is nice."

"Vincent does this whole romantic vibe thing. He opened this place decades ago. Even in Powers, it's a bit of a hidden spot."

"Little." A quiet yet booming voice had him jerking his gaze up—way up.

A massive man with beautiful coppery skin and the palest blue eyes he'd ever seen stood beside the table. He was dressed in tattered jeans and a black t-shirt, with a bandana wrapped around his head.

He realized he was staring when Harmon cleared his throat, and he turned to apologize, but Harmon's eyes shimmered with amusement. As Harmon shook his head, the man stood and wrapped the larger man in a tight hug. He noticed a similarity in the two men. The stranger seemed to relax at the embrace even as his skin darkened with a bit of embarrassment.

"Vincent, this is my Poe."

"It's very nice to meet you," Vincent whispered shyly as Harmon released him and turned toward him.

"Same, Vincent, you have a beautiful place."

"I'll make you two something special." Vincent spoke so quickly his words flowed into one, took the menus and escaped.

"Interesting man."

"Vincent is a bit of a hermit. He doesn't come out of his kitchen much. People make him nervous. You seemed to think he was pretty."

He took Harmon's hands back in his and leaned his forearms on the table. "No one is as handsome as you, Harmon."

"Dude, my ego isn't that fragile. Vincent gets that reaction a lot."

"Doesn't seem to like it though."

"He doesn't." Harmon's features grew serious. "I didn't really want to bring this up on the date, but if I don't go ahead and do it, I'm gonna forget."

"Then get it out."

"If you don't hear from me for a few days or you just want an update on where I am, I want you to go to Trenton. I made it clear they answer all your questions."

For some reason, Harmon was more nervous about this upcoming assignment. His man had gone away a few times since they'd met, but Harmon always called or texted every day—sometimes several messages.

"What aren't you telling me?"

He knew from their meeting with Trevor how sick of a man Carrington was, and he couldn't shake off the bad feeling he had. He loved Harmon, and that meant he had to be understanding—supportive. That was hard to do when he worried about Harmon getting hurt one day.

"It's not that I'm not telling you anything. I just don't want to lose you. You don't hide that you're not comfortable with my job."

"It's your life, Harmon, and I'll be here when you're home. Okay?"

Harmon nodded, but he knew his man wasn't satisfied with his answer. Harmon was very much about action because he had trusted empty words and promises too many times over the years. That was the frustrating part about being with Harmon. He kept wanting to tell Harmon everything he felt for the man, but in his heart and gut, he knew it was too soon.

"I know words don't mean much, baby, but all I can do is promise that I'm here for the long haul. You're mine, but more importantly, I'm yours."

"Okay, Poe."

"Now, let's have our romantic dinner and then I can take you home. Then I can love on you until you have to go to work tomorrow. Deal?"

"Really good deal."

He brought Harmon's hands to his mouth, kissed his man's scarred knuckles and loved how Harmon relaxed under his attention. Tomorrow was coming no matter how much he didn't want to say goodbye even for a short time. He'd be waiting. He didn't care how long it took.

WOULD HE SURVIVE?

*H*e hated the lead up to undercover assignments. Once he was in, everything was fine. This time was different though. He hated being locked up, and he wasn't looking forward to when the walls started to close in around him. Participating in treatment was also a danger. He knew he wasn't normal, but he didn't think he was crazy. But what was the saying, only the sane ones knew they were crazy?

He took a deep drag off his joint and studied the clinic across the street.

"Do you really have to do that right now?"

Hayden Gage glared at him from the driver's seat of the man's mid-life crisis classic Corvette. The man rolled down the window which defeated the purposes since it drew the smoke toward Gage.

"Man, I'm getting locked up. Let me have a minute."

They lapsed into silence as he finished smoking. He savored that heaviness of his limbs and the peace that infused him. He'd left drugs and alcohol behind nearly a decade ago. Weed was how he relaxed and found his center, his form of meditation. He remembered too much without the haze of liquor or the rush of cocaine through his veins. Fearlessness and stupidity colored his past, and at thirty-two, he'd finally found his way—his man.

"You know, you'll have eyes on you as much as we can."

"Doesn't matter when I'm in lockdown inside Carrington."

The claustrophobia was what worried him the most. He could take the treatments but being trapped caused him to break out in a cold sweat.

"Little, you don't have to do this. We all know this might fuck with your head."

"But ain't I the perfect one for this? I can take whatever they dish out." The bravado was false, and Gage knew it, he was sure of it.

"You have a partner now. When we get people of our own, it changes how we go about our jobs. We're more cautious about the moves we make."

"Is that why you cut down on working in the field?"

Gage had pulled back from the takedowns and the dangerous field work steadily over the last few years. They had thought he'd met someone, but Gage was as much alone as he always was. Out of everyone on the Trenton team, Gage was the one no one knew much about. The older man didn't give away his secrets easily. Hell, Gage didn't confess at all.

"No, a boy isn't meant for me."

"Aw." He threw his arms around Gage and hugged him tightly, giving the man a loud kiss on his bearded cheek. "I'd be your boy if I wasn't already Poe's."

"Get the fuck off me." Gage couldn't hide his chuckle as he pushed him away.

"You know you want it. Don't deny it." He let his fingertips dance along Gage's thigh and snorted as Gage smacked his hand.

"I'd spend too much time correcting you."

"You say that like it wouldn't be fun. I know you've checked out my ass."

Gage raised his hand to scrub his face and groaned. "Not in this lifetime, Little. You're so not my type."

"And what makes me not your type?"

"You're too bratty."

"I thought Daddies liked when their littles were bratty."

"I'm not having this conversation with you."

"You're no fun. Almost a prude. Everyone else talks about sex. You never—"

"That's because sex is personal and intimacy isn't to be taken lightly. When I find my partner, they'll know they're loved and respected, my only desire to make sure they're happy and safe."

"While putting them in the corner for a timeout."

"Get the fuck out of my car."

He grabbed his ratty old backpack from the floorboard between his feet. Inside was a few days of his worst looking clothes. An old expired ID. Half used travel sized personal items, and three condoms probably well past their expiration date. With Hunter's help, to the world, Harmon Little was just another homeless man with nowhere else to go.

"Here." Gage held up a small bag with a gram of white powder inside.

"Do I even want to know where you got that from?"

"Probably not, but you're going in there. They're going to search your bag."

"What if they call the cops instead of—"

"If what they're doing is true then they won't want the cops involved. Besides you have the best lawyer in the country, maybe beyond."

"True." He palmed the bag and stuffed it inside the pack through the broken zipper.

"We got your back. One twitch of the eye and we'll have you out."

He nodded and got out of the car, but before he jogged across the street, he looked both ways. Then he tugged his baseball cap down over his eyes.

Escape or extraction wouldn't be as easy as Gage made it out to be. They wouldn't have eyes in there. His GPS tag would only do so much. He could only hope they didn't confiscate everything when they admitted him.

He shoved a hand into his pocket, rubbed the pinch of pepper between his fingers to gather the oil. He brought his hand up to his nose. A sneeze built and his eyes watered, he slumped his shoulders and forced himself to shake. Being sick was his way in, but there was only so far he would go for his job.

He kept his head down as he entered but checked the waiting room from the corners of his eyes. Too many familiar faces barely looked his way. The hopeless aura was tangible and oppressive. Trevor's words came back to him. Carrington offered options to people who didn't believe they had any. The idea gilded and shiny.

"May we help you?" A woman with kind eyes stepped up beside him and hugged his waist—a bit of support. A caring he inherently knew was false.

"I—I have nowhere else to go."

"You don't have to worry about that, come with me?"

He was led back to a cramped office. He tilted his head back to study the brown water stains on the ceiling. He answered all the questions. From what he'd found out, he was the perfect candidate for Carrington's program. Brown. Homeless. He was a no one who appeared alone in the world, and that made him an easy target.

Not long ago he was just like everyone in that waiting room. Lost and looking for salvation, people to love and care if he lived or died. He had his teammates, friends, Lily and Damon, and now he had Poe.

He knew he'd have to participate in the solo and group

sessions. He didn't want to talk about his past. All the things and people who had broken him.

"We have a few openings at Dr. Carrington's clinic." Her soft hand gently touched his forearm. "I'm positive that we can help you. All you have to do is want the help...the chance to be better."

He knew that tone. It was equal parts placating and condescending. Like the woman was talking to a child. The soothing quality made him think of all the women who had used that soft voice to get him into bed.

"I want to be better." His words shuddered as he twitched and clenched his fists.

"Good, good, why don't we find you a place to lie down while I call the facility."

He allowed the woman to lead him to a room with a few gurneys pushed up to the walls on either side of the room. He hugged his bag to his chest as he eased onto one of them and stretched out. The lights clicked off, and he was left alone. With his eyes closed, he let his mind formulate escape routes. Memorized faces. Distinguishing marks. The more focused he became, the calmer he was.

He pretended to be asleep as he heard the door open, noticed a flare of light and at the prick of a needle, he started to fight. A big man in all black held him off. His movements became clumsy even as adrenaline coursed through his blood. He stumbled and the punch he threw barely grazed off the stranger's broad jaw.

He didn't catch himself in time, and the metal of the gurney's frame cut into his ribs. He shook his head in rough jerks as he tried to clear the fuzzy feeling.

Was Gage still outside?

Would he survive?

WHAT DID THEY DO TO HIS MAN?

$\mathcal{D}$ ays had passed, and he still reached for his phone to text Harmon. Still went to his place every night to sleep in his bed. Harmon had given him the code and the key. He didn't know if he had the right to demand information from Harmon's team or boss. Harmon had told them on their last night together that he'd told his team that they were to answer any of his questions. Too much time had gone by, and he didn't like not knowing if his man was okay. Harmon warned him. Yet he hadn't completely understood until his phone didn't ring or chime with just a message to say Harmon was safe.

That's why he was sitting outside Trenton Security and nervously watched the building.

Screw this, Harmon was his, and he wasn't going to sit there and not know what was going on with his man.

He opened his door and exited, he adjusted his bow tie and strode to the door. He pulled it open and entered an empty reception area. No one sat behind the huge reception desk.

"You're Little's man."

He jumped as a husky, male voice came over the PA system and he looked around.

"Go to the elevator and get off on the fourth floor. It's to the left."

He followed the directions, and the door opened as he reached it. He was barely in before the doors closed, and he was on the trip upward. He'd only met Fielding, Livingston, and Linus briefly. He hadn't recognized the voice. The door opened, and a friendly face met him. The man was tall and soft looking.

"Hi, I'm Hunter."

"You're one of Linus' husbands."

"Yes, I am, and you're Poe. Please come in. Did you want something to drink?"

He stepped out of the elevator and listened to the soft sound of the doors closing behind him.

"No, I haven't heard from Harmon, and I'm getting worried."

"You showed up in time for a meeting. I'm sure they wouldn't mind you sitting in."

"I wouldn't want to be a bother."

"Partners and husbands get priority around here."

A blond boy who looked to be pre-teen leaned against Hunter's side.

"This is Pride, our pain in the ass kid."

"Dad, I want to meet Ricky and Sawyer at Uncle Ben's."

"Means you need cash for your sugar fix."

"Yep."

"That didn't really require an answer, and since you picked my pocket, you weren't waiting for permission anyway."

He laughed at the roll of pale, almost translucent blue eyes and the kid produced a wallet with a magician's flare.

"You have to stop hanging out with Raul. I don't think my twelve-year-old needs to know how to pick a pocket or hotwire a car."

"Uncle Raul says—"

He recognized names from the stories Harmon told him. Raul was a freelancer turned full-time member of Trenton. Everyone seemed to believe that Raul had a thing for Pure. He hadn't remembered a time when he'd laughed so much when Harmon would relay all the weird stories to him.

"I don't need to know what your Uncle Raul says. You need friends more your age."

"Did I mention I want to hang with Ricky and Sawyer?"

He stood there as he watched the exchange of money and the kid batted at Hunter to get away without being the victim of fatherly affection. When the elevator doors open and closed behind him, he listened to Hunter's deep sigh.

"He shouldn't be allowed to hang around the office. I'll take you to the conference room."

He followed the bigger man down a long hallway toward large double doors. Hunter gave a quick knock and then just walked inside. A group of huge men turned including the local Sheriff and a heavily tattooed woman in an expensive suit. He nodded at Livingston who had Fielding on his lap, and the man's husband had his head rested on Livingston's shoulder.

Hunter broke away from him and strode toward Linus. They shared a quick kiss.

"You're Little's." The woman was in motion and had him pulled into her arms. "I'm Peaches. Little's been keeping you all to himself. My boys have never learned to share their partners' time."

Warmth infused his cheeks in pleasure at being called Harmon's so easily.

"I think it's more I don't like sharing Harmon."

"Good boy, Little needed someone."

"I haven't heard from Harmon in days, and I'm getting worried."

"We're just getting ready to start our meeting. Have a seat. Don't hesitate to ask questions."

He took in her serious expression and nodded, as he found a seat everyone introduced themselves.

"Since we have a new arrival let's back up a bit. What's the situation?" Linus gave Hunter one last squeeze, and Hunter took the chair at the head of the long conference table. "Gage?"

"Our man outside Carrington hasn't spotted Little since he entered the facility. Patients are allowed out late afternoon. None of them have been Little."

"What about his GPS tags?" he asked.

That was the reason he was nervous. Harmon had wanted to put him at ease and set him up with a tracker to go along with the tags so he'd know where Harmon was while he was away. He'd thought it strange when Harmon had plopped down on the bed beside him the morning he'd left. He'd listened carefully as Harmon explained everything to him.

"Tags?" Pure asked.

"Yeah, he took a book with him. He had about four flesh colored tags hidden in the spine plus the one he was wearing when he'd left home."

"Sneaky fucker. He didn't tell us about those."

"The app he put on my phone hasn't pinged me with his location since the day after he left."

That was the moment he'd started to worry. Harmon was too concerned with making him happy. He knew his man still waited for the day he'd grow tired of Harmon. It didn't matter how many times he'd told Harmon he had no intention of leaving. He knew it was quick, but he was in love with Harmon. Wanted to build a life with him.

"May I see your phone?"

He nodded as he leaned back to pull his phone from his pocket and handed it to Hunter.

"They may have confiscated what he brought in. He was holding when he was admitted. I gave him a gram of coke for his cover."

"Gage." Pelter groaned and scrubbed his hands over his face.

They seemed a little too free with illegal activities with the Sheriff in on the meeting.

"It was for his cover. Fuck, it's not like he put it up his nose."

"I don't want to hear it. I overlook the weed bullshit, but I can't—"

"Like you haven't been in possession of illegal substances in your line of work."

As he turned his head, he grinned at Peaches when he found her cross-legged and barefoot sitting on the opposite end of the table.

"Not the point, Peaches."

"Exactly the point. Just because you have a badge, Mr. Law and Order, doesn't make you better than my—"

"Can we get back to work?" Linus asked.

Peaches motioned for Linus to go ahead.

"What do we know? Gage?"

"We arrived at the free clinic. A van pulled up out front about twenty minutes after Little went in and I waited half an hour to see if he came out. When he didn't, I returned to the office. Hunter ran the plates, and they came back registered to Carrington's facility."

"We're trying to get someone inside, but their policy is newly admitted patients are on lockdown while they go through detox." No one could miss the frustration in Linus' voice.

"Harmon's not addicted to anything."

"He's been around enough he can fake that shit," Raul said as he shifted in his chair.

"I can get a court order to get someone in, but I think the only one who could pull it off is Poe here. Estranged husband, maybe ex-husband." Peaches said.

"Baby, you think you can take care of that?"

"It's like you doubt my skills." Hunter was strangely cute when he pouted up at Linus. "Poe, I'm going to snatch your phone for a few minutes to take to my office."

Hunter was already in motion without waiting for an answer. He didn't think any of the Trenton team cared much about rules.

"Hunter will get all the paperwork set up. Peaches will go in as your lawyer."

He glanced at Linus. "What do I do? Just demand to see him?"

"Carrington doesn't want heat brought down on his operation. There's too much money funneling through his organization. The fucker is crazy enough to believe using street kids or junkies for his research that he's coming up with miracle cures. The rich will do anything to fix their embarrassments."

It was the *anything* that frightened him the most. He didn't like thinking about his man as fragile, but Harmon was exactly that. They'd broken Harmon down too early in life. Caused him to feel unworthy and unlovable.

Was Harmon safe?

"Hey." A soft but strong hand took his and gave it a reassuring squeeze—Peaches. "Little will be fine. He's got you and us. It's not easy for the partners when their men leave, but Little is great at his job. He also has someone very important to come home to, and that will get him through."

"I hope so. I worry. I just got him, and I'm not ready to lose him now or any time soon."

"You won't. Lily and I want Little back, these boys of ours don't want to fuck with us. We're not losing a kid."

He forced a smile, but he wasn't sure. That wasn't the life he knew anything about. His and Harmon's times together were at the warehouse. The two of them learning about each other. He wanted his man back and soon.

* * *

HE RUBBED his sweaty palms along his thighs as he sat in the back of a nondescript sedan. The ring on his left hand felt off and heavy. It wasn't that he was averse to wearing a wedding ring one day, but it wasn't the type he thought Harmon would give him. He shouldn't be thinking about that. A week passed since he'd seen or heard from Harmon. They'd worked quickly and gotten the cover in place within a few days.

Gage drove while he was in the back with Peaches. She kept touching his hand. Offering him words of comfort that he didn't want to hear. It wasn't that he didn't appreciate it because he did.

His head was all fucked-up. Things had changed so much over the past few months. His determination to change to fit what he thought was desirable had damn near become an obsession. Then he'd met a sweet and odd man who changed how he looked at himself and his decisions.

Yes, he didn't like things about himself. Everyone did; it was human nature. He felt more confident. More himself. He'd found his place—his person. He didn't know how he felt about Harmon's job, but his man seemed to love it. Although, what happened on this job wouldn't be occurring again. He couldn't handle being out of contact. Not knowing if his Harmon was safe.

He jerked his gaze to Gage as the man pulled to a stop in front of a high gate.

"Can I help you, sir?" A big guy in a generic security company uniform leaned down to look around the inside of the car.

"We're here to see Harmon Little. He was brought in about a week ago."

"You're not on the approved list."

"We have a court order that allows Mr. Little's husband to see the patient. I can make a call to the local police and have them come out to help us execute the order."

He didn't miss the tightening of the man's square jaw.

"I'll call up to the office."

The man straightened and went into the small glass-enclosed booth. It didn't appear the guard was too happy about the conversation he was having.

His legs bounced nervously as his brain decided to come up with everything that could go wrong.

The guard simply stuck his head past the door as the gate started to open.

"Dr. Carrington will meet you out front."

Gage didn't respond simply put the car into gear and drove forward. Then taking a left to make the trip around the circular drive. He looked up at the building as they slowed and a middle-aged man in a suit waited at the top of the steps. The man's hands pushed deep into his pockets, and his expression gave nothing away.

"I'll do all the talking, but if he asks you questions, keep the answers short and simple."

He nodded at Peaches, and then Gage was opening her door and helping her out. He noticed she wore an outfit that hid most of her tattoos and the scarf around her neck concealed the ones there. He sensed she didn't like concealing them. She'd told him the story to distract him earlier about what every tattoo meant. Anniversary presents from her husband, Gib. He surprised her with a design on the milestones including their first date, when she'd said yes to marrying him, and on the date they had married. The designs lovingly created and inked into her skin by her husband of over four decades.

He was jerked from his musings when Gage opened the door for him. He got out and smoothed his gray suit, adjusted his new yellow bow tie. He knew his man would love it. It made his man blissful, and it was such a small thing. Harmon didn't demand much for himself, to be touched and kissed, held and cuddled. Harmon didn't seem to require more than that.

"Dr. Carrington, I presume." Peaches' voice was cold and professional.

"Yes, I believe I'm at a disadvantage."

"This is my associate, Hayden Gage, and my client, Solomon Poe. I'm Veronica Phelps."

"I believe you told my guard that Mr. Poe was the husband of a patient of mine."

"It's an odd situation. They've been separated due to Mr. Little's mental state for a few years, but Mr. Poe's husband never goes without making contact with him."

"Clinic policy is our patients aren't allowed visitors while they go through the detox process. Which I'm sure you're aware can be a rather tiring and sometimes dangerous procedure."

"Mr. Little didn't inform his husband that he'd be admitting himself to a facility."

"Is that a fact, Mr. Poe?"

"Yes, Harmon and I have an understanding. I love him very much, and while he works through his...issues, I only require he make contact."

"He's at a delicate stage of his treatment. As his physician I—"

Peaches cut the man off with a cheery smile, and he was amazed at how calm she was. Over the last few days as they planned how they'd go about getting into see Harmon, he'd seen her flashes of temper. Her Mama Bear attitude when she went toe-to-toe with men who looked scarier than her. He'd felt sorry for Linus and Gage, even Livingston a few times.

"I respect your professional opinion, but we secured a court order. As my associate mentioned to the guard at the gate, we can contact the local authorities. We'd prefer not to bring attention to the matter. Mr. Poe would simply like to spend a few minutes with his husband to make sure he's okay and wants to be here. Mr. Poe is hoping they can reconcile once Mr. Little is released."

"Very well, but as I've examined and talked to Mr. Little at length. I believe his stay here will be beneficial to his long-term health both mental and physical."

He gritted his teeth to avoid calling the man a liar. There was nothing wrong with his man. To him, Harmon was perfect just the way he was and that bastard talking about—he ordered himself to calm down and take deep breaths. He couldn't mess this up. They needed to see Harmon.

"Why don't you come in and I'll have one of my assistants get you some refreshments. We'll get Mr. Little moved to a private visiting room."

"As I am Mr. Little's attorney along with Mr. Poe, I require that any monitoring be turned off during the visit. Even though we're here to make sure Mr. Little is okay, there's a few legal matters that we need to discuss as well."

"As you wish, but with Mr. Little's volatile nature, I believe it—"

"Mr. Gage is also my private security. He's more than capable of handling Mr. Little. As I said, client-attorney confidentiality is paramount."

He knew Peaches had a signal jammer in her purse that would ensure their meeting was private, but by Carrington's reaction, he didn't like the fact he wouldn't get to listen in. They knew he was hiding something. He knew they had enough evidence to prove it.

Everything seemed to move in slow motion as they were set up in a room with coffee and tea. He'd requested a bottle of apple juice for Harmon. He laced his fingers as he waited on an uncomfortable wooden chair. The walls were stark white and the afternoon sun blazed through a single, small window.

He'd studied the place as Carrington had led them through the facility to the room. It looked very upscale. Hotel-esque with a hint of a spa retreat. He'd never seen that many diamonds in his life. Most of them were dressed in fancy yet casual clothes. He didn't notice one patient who didn't look like someone he'd meet at one of his parents' parties. It was all for show. Probably to mask the horrors of what really happened there.

He surged to his feet and spun toward the door as soon as he heard the knob turn. His eyes filled with tears. Harmon's face was drawn and ashen, he seemed thinner. His hands clenched at his sides until the orderly seated Harmon and backed out of the room.

The orderly said he'd be right outside and then they were left alone. He rushed forward, and Harmon didn't even look at him.

"Baby." His voice broke as he took Harmon's face into his hands. The man's beard was thick and scraggly, his hair growing out.

"What the fuck did they do? It's been seven fucking days!" Gage was enraged, but he ignored the man.

Harmon didn't acknowledge them, and he glanced over his shoulder to see Peaches covering her mouth, tears streaming down her cheeks.

"Harmon." He kissed Harmon's dry, cracked lips. There wasn't a response. Harmon always responded to affection. "Baby, you're worrying me."

Harmon's green eyes were dull and lifeless as if his man wasn't in there. What did they do to his man?

WAS ANY OF IT REAL?

"*I told you I loved you just for a fuck, man.*"
    "*Who could want a thing like you?*"
"*You weren't worth the fifty, kid.*"
"*Mama, mama. Take me with you.*"

Each word pierced his skull with blinding pain. A breeze across his skin was like he was on fire. He was an atheist, but at that moment he believed in Hell. He categorized everything. Took stock of toes, fingers, limbs, counted every breath as he tried to pull himself back from the edge. He didn't know what they'd given him.

He'd awakened strapped to a cot in a windowless room. The mustiness of mold and sharpness of antiseptic burned his nose as his brain slowly cleared. He had fought against the restraints until he realized it was futile. Then he'd taken an inventory of the room which didn't take long. His bag was missing, and the only furniture in the room was the cot.

The mystery injections started not long after he came to and then the interrogations followed. Questions to check did he know what year it was or what was his first memory. How did he feel? Was he experiencing hallucinations? Was it a repeat of the same questions to make sure his answers matched? To make sure they weren't frying the last of his brain cells.

He closed his eyes and tried to push away the evil shit filling his head. Poe. His man's soft lips brushing against his cheek to wake him in the mornings. The curve of Poe's smile against his skin.

"You're going to get tired of me being here every morning."

He combed his fingers through Poe's silky hair. "Never happen."

"Have I told you how happy I am you ran into me?"

"Maybe, I can't remember. Refresh my memory."

He jerked as the sting of another needle forced him away from his happy place. He felt outside himself. Disconnected and numb. He couldn't even bring himself to fight as he felt the restraints loosen and he was pulled to his feet. His body moved involuntarily. Taking the lead from the person holding his arm. His eyes stung from the brightness as he was led up a set of stairs. When had he seen sunlight last? How long had he been locked up?

Time stood still. Passing only in a repetition of injections and questionings.

His body felt so heavy, and he could barely keep his eyes open. He just wanted to go to sleep and dream of Poe. Have his man love on him one more time. He feared he wasn't going to make it out. How long would his team wait to rescue him and would he still be him when it happened?

He was pushed down into a chair, and he prepared himself to answer the same set of questions, wondering if his answers would be the same or had they finally turned his brain to mush.

Soft, gentle hands touched his face—Poe's hands. Then he heard the sweetest sound—Poe's voice. If only it was real and not a product of his drugged mind.

"Baby."

Poe's voice broke. He didn't like when his man was sad. Poe should always be perky and smiling.

"*What the fuck did they do? It's been seven fucking days?*"

What was Gage doing in his hallucination? He only wanted Poe. Poe made him safe.

"*Harmon.*"

Poe's plump lips touched his so tenderly, but he couldn't respond. His body wouldn't listen to him. He loved Poe's kisses, and his man did it a lot. Quick ones in passing or while he worked. Then there were the ones Poe gave him while they lay in bed or curled up on the couch. He held onto the memories of Poe filling him as his man whispered loving words in his ear. He wanted to go home to Poe. He didn't want to be there anymore.

"*Baby, you're worrying me.*"

He jerked as arms wrapped around his neck and he felt himself flinch.

"*Harmon Little, you never flinch from me. Do you understand me?*"

Oh shit, his Poe was mad at him.

He opened his mouth to say he was sorry, but nothing came out. He clenched his hands on his thighs, and then the familiar weight of Poe crawled onto his lap. Warm puffs of air teased his ear.

"*Baby, our bed isn't the same without you in it with me.*"

He missed Poe's cuddles. He needed this to be real. He needed his man with him and forced heavy eyelids open, the flash of blinding light sent agony through his head. His brow furrowed and he tried again. His vision was nothing more than floating halos; then it began to clear. What he saw was distorted by double vision. First, he saw Gage ringed in a bright aura. Next was Peaches and tears shimmered like diamonds on her cheeks.

"Little, you with us, man?"

Gage's face turned into a blur as the man leaned in close. He didn't like the roughness of Gage's hands on his face and the tug of the man's thumbs just under his eyes. It forced his eyes open more than the slit he was using to block out the brightness of the room. He jerked his head back and finally Poe's beautiful face came into focus.

"Raul's been checking out your boy."

"Are you trying to piss him off?" Peaches asked with a groan. "A pissed off Little isn't exactly sane."

"When is Little sane?"

"Could you not talk about my man like he isn't here?"

My man. He'd never get tired of hearing that even if right then was nothing more than a dream.

"I'm trying to piss him off. A bit of adrenaline to clear his head. He's way too calm. Hey, Little, ever thought about sharing your boy. I bet he'd be so pretty collared and on his—"

He felt the give of flesh and tendons beneath the strength of his grip. The world was still out of focus, but rage drove some of that away. Poe was his. No one would take him away.

Gage gurgled and rasped as the man tried to breathe with his hand around his throat.

"Mine." The words rasped almost painfully up his throat.

"All yours, big man."

He relaxed as Poe soothed him with words and touches, the things he'd missed. How long had he been away? Panic tightened his chest as he felt it all begin to drift away.

"Hey, baby, stay with me, look me in the eyes, handsome."

He obeyed the order and stared right into pretty eyes hidden behind the cute thick-framed glasses. His mouth pulled up at the corners as he pictured the way Poe squinted when he took them off. His man couldn't see shit.

"I want to go home."

"I know, and I want you home. What did they do to you?"

His mind didn't want to function, and his head hurt the more he tried to force it.

"Shots. Lots of shots. My body on fire. So hard to stay present."

"It's okay. You'll be coming home. You need a shave and a haircut…you're all scruffy. Well, maybe, it's sexy as fuck."

Part of him knew what Poe was doing. His man attempted to keep him grounded which was exactly what the man had done since they met. He was lost without Poe. He was safe and loved, he wanted to hear his man tell him, but Poe hadn't said it yet. Was Poe just temporary?

The sharp agony of fear dragged him closer to the abyss where he'd fall again. He didn't want to plunge into the darkness again. He could feel the specter of the razor again. The one he'd slowly stroked over his forearms years ago. The marks were hidden under the dark ink that covered his arms wrists to shoulders. He didn't tell anyone about those. Hadn't even told Poe because he didn't want his man to look at him differently.

If Poe knew just how fucked-up he was, then the man he loved wouldn't stay. Poe was like Lily, they made everything better and let him stay in the present where he wasn't mired by the past. His past didn't matter. His impulse control bullshit didn't matter.

"Little, you gotta look at me," Gage's order snapped him to attention. "We're going to have to leave you."

"No, I want to go—"

"I know, man, you want to go home, and that's exactly where you're going, but I have to call in the team. Tell me how many paces from here to where your room is? Were there stairs? How many paces from the stairs is your room? We need this information, and we need it now."

He threw his head forward as Gage slapped his face. If he were in control, he would've broken the bastard's nose. He closed his eyes, dug through the dark and tried to retrace his steps. He played the scene in reverse, but he couldn't be sure. What if the information was all a figment of his imagination? Maybe this meeting—

"You're fading on me." Gage guttural voice hit him hard.

He relayed the information as clearly as he could. It could be off, but all they needed was a general idea of where he was kept.

"I don't care what you have to do, Little, you be ready to fight or run. You have a man to go home to, do you understand me?"

"Yes, sir."

"We gotta go, I can't contact the team from in here. Remember, survive at all costs."

He knew leaving a man behind for Gage was the worst failure a leader could experience.

"Harmon, Lily sent a present for you, but you don't get it until you come home."

"I just want you. Please don't leave me."

"Baby, I'll be waiting, promise me you'll fight."

Emotion closed down his throat, and he couldn't speak; all his body would allow was him hiding his face against the side of Poe's neck.

"Come on, Harmon, let Poe go, you'll see him soon. I promise."

He started to sob as Peaches' arms joined Poe's around him. He held onto them tight even as they pulled away. The tears flowed down his cheeks, but he didn't care. They were leaving him just like everyone left.

"Harmon Little, I love you, and I will say that in a more romantic setting soon. You have to get home to me, remember?"

He had stopped breathing at the word love and terror took over. Poe's *I love you* collided with the past ones. The pretty lies whispered in tones that hid the falsehood of them. But Poe didn't want anything from him. He didn't demand sex. Poe had held him as they fell asleep more than they'd fucked.

"Harmon, stay with me."

"Yes, Poe." He opened his mouth to say it, but Poe's lips were pressed to his.

"You say it when your head is clear."

Poe held his face in his small hands, and he held tight to Poe's wrists. He fought Gage when the man tried to pull Poe away from him, but then the strange cologne mixed with cigarette smoke he remembered from the orderly overwhelmed him. He'd promised to fight, but how long could he hold off the next needle?

He was weak and confused by the drugs, and he felt as if he'd lost weight. He could fight. He'd get home. He refused to die in that fucking windowless room.

THEY NEEDED TO GET HIS MAN
OUT NOW

*T*he few hours that he'd slept was filled with nightmares of Harmon broken and alone. The entire Trenton team along with a few strange faces filled a cramped motel room. They had Gibson, the Powers Fire Chief, who had medic training, on hand for any emergencies. Then there were two scary men named Horace and Freddie who looked as if they'd just escaped from a mental ward or prison, maybe both. He didn't think they should be in possession of firearms. Gage called in a friend of his, Alex, and the man was wearing a suit that screamed money.

Alex was all polished and elegant, a blond Adonis Daddy with silver-streaked hair among the sea of heathens in black tactical gear.

He didn't know half the stuff they were talking about. He could figure out most of it, though. Once the operation went down, Pelter and Peaches would handle local law enforcement.

"You doing okay, Poe?"

Hunter sat down beside him in one of the stained chairs. The place looked like it should come with a dose of antibiotics along with the key to get into the room.

"He looked so bad." His man was strong and most of the time

had a smile on his face. When Harmon had said he wanted to go home, he'd wanted to bundle his man up right then. It hadn't sat well with him when they'd left him behind. Gage explained they didn't know what kind of security the clinic had. It turned out that the clinic had a crew of ex-special forces who took care of problems. He still didn't know how they were going to get Harmon out.

"From what Gage told us, he looked dehydrated and underfed."

"Gage said he needed to be ready to fight. He could barely lift his arms."

"Little knows his job. Instinct will kick in, and he'll know what to do," Hunter said.

The rational side of him told him that these men were far more experienced at this sort of thing than he was. Although, the other part was terrified that everything would go wrong. That the last time he'd see his man breathing was in that tiny visiting room.

"What are they talking about?"

"They're looking at the best points of entry. I was able to get my hands on the blueprints, and I hacked into the records. Our client's mother isn't listed as a patient, but the names that were, are the who's who of the infamous. There's a few FBI's most wanted inside. Carrington sure as fuck doesn't want to draw attention."

"Wouldn't it be stupid to use real names?"

"They didn't. I cross-referenced aliases and a few matched up. Some people have more money than brains. Peaches recognized a few names and said they wouldn't be problems."

"How would she know?"

"She'd have to kill you and me if I told you."

As Hunter laughed his ass off, he returned his attention to his laptop. Since he'd met Peaches, he'd noticed that the woman seemed to be in charge. Pissing her off was to be avoided at all costs, but when he'd seen her cry, it terrified him. The woman was too fucking strong to break down.

"Poe," Linus called his name, and then the man crouched down in front of him. "We're setting up with body cams so that you can be there every step of the way. You're going to see shit you don't like, but you gotta keep it together for when we bring Little out. You got me?"

"Yes. Is he going to be okay?"

"If not, then we're going to have bodies to answer for. We get you didn't like leaving him behind. It wasn't what we fucking wanted either, but safety is top priority. Especially when it comes to one of my team."

"I just want him home."

He was surprised when Linus took his hands and squeezed them.

"Listen, we're getting Little out no matter what we have to fucking do. You'll be in the van about a mile from the facility. Horace and Freddie will be on you at all times."

He peeked around Linus at the two men in question. "Are they safe?" he whispered. Both men were burly, not overly tall, but Horace had a darkness in his eyes, and his heavily silver-streaked long hair hung to conceal the harsh angles of his face. Freddie was the same height but wider through the shoulders and chest. They both had ink covering their arms. Violent slashes of crimson and what looked like crushed skulls like a massacre. Horace had more skulls than Freddie and wondered if there was a reason for that, but he felt it wouldn't be safe to ask.

Linus snorted. "Safe, yes, sane, not so much."

He rolled his eyes and pushed against Linus' chest. "You're not being very comforting."

"I wouldn't leave them with you if I thought they'd put you in danger or be a danger to you. Little trusts them. I didn't think he'd mind them being around his man."

Linus' voice was soft, almost caring. He was used to hearing the word fuck come out of Linus' mouth about every other word. He also didn't forget the blows Liv and Linus exchanged the other day while they were having a *friendly* match.

When had his life become a SWAT reality show episode?

He slumped into the chair and sighed as he rubbed his hands over his face.

"You got Little's kit ready?"

"I got Lily's present and his favorite energy drinks."

"He's so fucking easy to please."

He smiled as he thought about Harmon. His man didn't need much. Some affection. His own space. He loved that Harmon wasn't like the men he'd met in the past. Harmon was unique and perfect. When he'd whispered that he loved Harmon, that wasn't the way he'd wanted to tell Harmon, but he'd needed his man to know. The agony that twisted Harmon's face had broken his heart. His man would never look that lost again.

* * *

ONE A.M. found him sitting in the back of Harmon's van in the ratty recliner he'd pulled up to the monitors mounted on the side. Each cam was assigned a screen, and the laptop let him zoom in, and he'd switched them to night vision. He listened to the chatter and whatever code they spoke was making his head hurt.

"What are they talking about?"

"They've breached the outer wall at the back of the facility. At this point, they don't see any guards walking the perimeter. Alex has eyes on the guard at the gate, and he'll take him out, then make an entrance at the front." Horace pointed at the screens he spoke.

It was a voice that sounded as if it wasn't used often.

"We're hoping for a soft entry and exit."

"And—"

He had the urge to elbow Freddie when the man grunted. "It means we're hoping for a quick in and out, you know like a bad fuck."

"Y'all don't get out very often, do you?"

"We live in the woods by ourselves," they answered in tandem.

"I am in no way surprised."

"Little doesn't spank you enough."

He couldn't help his snort/laugh hybrid at Freddie's disgusted tone. Harmon hadn't even attempted to spank him, but Harmon loved to receive a spanking. In no way was he complaining about that. He didn't care how open they were about sex; he wasn't going to be one of them to talk easily about it.

"Linus and Liv are at the back exit."

"Baby, is the system down." Linus' voice filled his earpiece.

Hunter responded, "Give me...got it. I'll lock it back down once you're in."

He closely watched the monitors as the team seemed to move in a practiced choreography. Seamless. He remembered they were going in at an employee access door to the basement level. The place was dark, and the paint was peeling from the walls. It was like one of those scenes people would see in horror movies about abandoned asylums.

"Alex, we good?"

"No movement. This fucking place is a ghost town."

His eyes widened at Mr. Three Piece Suit popping out an F-bomb.

"Don't sound so disappointed," Gage sounded amused.

"Teams of two. Room by room search until we find our targets. Silence except for five-minute check-ins."

The targets were Harmon and the client's mother.

"Gentleman, you have an hour before rounds," Hunter informed them.

His legs bounced as his eyes darted to each monitor. It was getting harder to keep track of who was who even though names were on the screen. He wanted to ask questions. Make demands, but he bit his tongue and perched on the edge of the seat.

"Their clearing all the rooms following a preplanned grid search."

He nodded at Horace's explanation. He didn't know why, but when they sat on the arms of the chair, and he felt their warmth, he found it strangely soothing. A few hours ago, he'd asked if it was safe to be trapped with them and there he was taking comfort in their presence.

A momentary crackling preceded Raul's voice. "Boss, we found our female target."

"Secure her. Any sighting of our second target?"

The echoing of no almost made him collapse. Where was Harmon? They needed to get his man out now.

SHOCK TREATMENTS AND SO-CALLED MIRACLES

An overwhelming repetition of voices blended into a horror-esque soundtrack—ominous and foreboding. Past and present stitched together in some macabre quilt that trapped him beneath its weight. The effects of the medicine were waning, but in no way eased his anxiety. His rough restraints dug into the abraded skin of his wrists and ankles. He'd come to the conclusion as he'd awakened to someone in a surgical mask wheeling him down a hallway that he wasn't going to make it out.

He counted the mesh-encased lights as he'd passed under them. Memorized the hard clunk of elevator doors and the whirr of an engine. He didn't know if he ascended or went deeper into the bowels of his nightmare.

Was any of it real?

Did he imagine his man was there?

Had Peaches cried over him?

Had his Poe said I love you? The words he'd always longed for a person to tell him but it hadn't been real. It was the poison they forced into his veins. He jerked his head in a sharp shake as if it would help clear out the residual effects of whatever they'd used to drug him.

Gage had told him he needed to be ready to fight. The attempt to lift his head—his limbs—seemed to take everything he had. His muscles tensed to the point of pain. That was the only thing he'd remembered—the agony. Suffering was the only sensation the injections hadn't numbed.

A shockingly white room with bright lights caused him to squint.

"Doctor, the subject is ready." A professional voice bordering on sweet sounded above him.

"Then let us begin."

Even in his haze, he recognized Carrington's voice.

How many others had the good doctor done this too? People not as physically strong as him, broken in unimaginable ways and only searching for salvation but only shattering further by the torture. Kids who only wished for a way out submitting to hollow promises.

His mouth was forced open, and something hard and gauze covered slipped between his teeth. He rolled his head to the side and even though it was fruitless, he started to fight at the sight of the machine beside the table.

Carrington started to speak again. Reciting the date and time. He'd been here ten days. He had lost so much time, and in his gut, he knew this was where it ended. No way was he getting out of this room alive.

"Subject two-nine-seven has responded well to the medication. The subject has shown to be receptive to suggestion, but now we move to phase two of treatment." Carrington announced the voltage.

As he bowed his body up from the gurney, he pulled with what was left of his strength at the tethers which held him down. His body was forced flat onto the gurney, and a strap came across his forehead. Even if the gag in his mouth wasn't keeping him from yelling and cursing, the thickness of his tongue and dryness of his throat choked him. Forced him into speechlessness, but he grunted. The sounds didn't convey his anger and, yes, fear of what was to come.

Icy gel was smeared onto his temples, and he held his breath, prepared for what was to come. Paddles pressed to his prepared skin and then it was like static shock times a thousand. His body lengthened and seized as the electricity coursed through him. His screams were muffled. His jaw clenched, and his teeth cut into the hard material between them.

As fast as it hit, the torture ceased, and he collapsed as his breath rushed in a trembling rhythm in and out through his nose. Then the next announcement came, and as prepared as he was, there was nothing he could do. He felt his eyes roll upward so fast that his muscles pulled. His frame pulled to the breaking point as the jolt hit him again.

Somewhere in the distance, he heard a crash and a woman yell. All he knew was the pain stopped, and he was thankful his mind could still formulate in a small way what was going on around him. A rough hand came across his face and anger took over.

The gag was removed from his mouth, and he felt it pull at his teeth where they'd sunk into it.

"Little, look at me, man." Liv's voice was too loud. "Open those eyes for me."

His eyelids felt like they were weighed down, but he forced them open as he listened to the shrill sound of *Velcro* giving.

"Linus, we found him."

"Come on, Little," Raul's voice whispered in his ear.

He was eased up and off the gurney, and his legs gave out under his weight.

"We have ten minutes to get to the exit point. Let's move."

He was too weak to make it. They should leave him behind.

"We're not leaving you behind. Poe is outside waiting for you. You going to leave your man to mourn your oversized ass?" Liv demanded.

Poe was there. His weight was leaned too heavily into Raul, but thankfully the man was able to hold him up. His vision was blurry, and his head seemed to float high above his shoulders. He picked a point and focused on it. He instinctively knew Pure was at his six but the rest of the team were in formation in front of him.

One second they were making their way down a corridor, and the next, he was on the floor. He turned his head as he heard the click of a weapon. To his left, his masked team stood there, teams of two, one knelt and the other standing. Weapons drawn. He forced his attention the other way and could only see through Raul's legs as the man shielded him.

He was useless. Gage had told him he'd need to fight, but he didn't have the energy or will to do so.

"You won't make it out of here."

Carrington's arrogance was clear as he stood there with the gun in his hand, but he noticed the slight shake. The man's confidence wasn't as strong as it appeared. Two guards had semi-automatic weapons aimed at them with the butts of the stock pushed into their shoulders. He wouldn't fucking go out without a fight.

He forced his arm upward until he removed Raul's sidearm from the man's thigh holster. His thumb flipped the safety off, and he took aim, he closed one eye and picked which version of Carrington to aim at.

"I wouldn't be so sure of that." Linus' voice held a dark, dangerous edge. "We have enough evidence to sink you and your torture chamber. Pure?"

"On your command."

It all happened in that slow-motion cinema effect, Carrington lifted the gun higher.

"Take them."

A quick, even bursts of gunfire filled the corridor, and the guards' bodies fell. Carrington still stood and defiantly glared at them. His mind cleared as everything shrunk to a hazy frame around Carrington. Adrenaline made him come back to himself. The doctor raised his arm, prepared to fire. He exhaled as he squeezed the trigger and the scent of gunpowder filled his nose. Carrington's arms flew out to the sides, and he collapsed. He didn't feel any guilt at the explosion of crimson in the middle of the man's forehead.

"Movement at the end of the hall," Gage announced and they spun as a single unit—the symbiotic relationship of a tight team.

He was suddenly on his feet, and Raul once again carried him. It was organized chaos as they cleared rooms and he felt like dead weight as his legs refused to hold him. His team—his family —wouldn't leave him behind. He wanted to get out. Needed to see his man again. His world would be back to normal as soon as his man was back in his arms.

It seemed like hours later before he felt the cool night air on his face and they were running into the darkness. Shouts filled the night, and more gunfire filled the once silent night.

The sharp sounds of shots came from somewhere in the distance, one, two, and then a third."

"Alex, meet at the extraction point," Linus ordered, and he wondered who Alex was, but he didn't have much time to contemplate. His left leg dragged, and pain traveled along his right. The adrenaline was waning too quickly.

"Harmon," Poe's voice called out to him.

He jerked his gaze around until he spotted his man running toward him and then Poe was on his other side helping Raul. His van came into view, and he found himself stashed inside. Too many bodies filled the cramped space, but it didn't expand into claustrophobia as Poe placed kisses all over his face. His man's soft hands moved over him as if searching for wounds.

"Baby, talk to me, are you okay?" Poe frantically whispered against his mouth.

He tried to get his tongue to work, but his body started to

float away, and his brain wouldn't form the words to soothe his man.

"Harmon," Poe cried his name. "We needed to get to a hospital."

Those were the last words he heard before everything shut down and he let the darkness take over.

* * *

THE STEADY BEAT of a heart monitor brought him back to the present. Once again, voices blended into an echo of one, but it didn't possess the fear-inducing atmosphere of the facility. He inherently sensed he was free and he lay there with his eyes closed. He searched his memory, and they started to come back to him slowly. The operation. His team was rescuing him. Poe.

"Kieran, why isn't he awake yet?" Poe's sweet voice sounded tired.

"They did a drug test, but without access to Carrington's files on Harmon's treatment, we can't be sure what they've injected him with. The doctor said his vitals are fine. Except for needing a few good meals and another bag of fluids, he's physically fine. Mentally, unless I get to talk to him, I won't know the extent of the damage done by what was essentially days of torture."

Then he remembered who Kieran was, Dr. Dahl was the local shrink. New guy in town. No one really knew much about him.

"Here's my card. When he's ready to make an appointment just call and set one up. With the number of injection marks, he might not remember much about what happened."

He flexed his fingers and toes, took stock of himself and while his entire body ached deep down in his bones everything appeared to work.

"But you can't guarantee that."

"What he needs right now is a lot of TLC. Make sure he gets plenty of rest. With the information you've given me about his past, he's going to have to process a lot. I'll be back tomorrow and check in."

"Thanks."

"You're welcome. Just take care of your man, and when it's time, I'll do my part."

He heard the sound of dress shoes on linoleum and then the soft whoosh of a door opening, then closing. The bed dipped beside his hip, and as the man laid his head on his chest, he absorbed Poe's warmth.

"Is this real?" His voice broke as he forced his heavy eyelids up.

"Oh, baby, it's real. You're finally awake."

He relished the soft kisses that landed all over his face, then Poe's mouth rested on his. As he tried to lift his arms to hold his man, they refused to move.

"Relax, you've been asleep for days."

"What happened?"

"Well, what do you remember?"

As he tried to piece everything together, he couldn't decide what was real or fantasy. Was this one of his *happy place* hallucinations?

"Not much."

"Well, you don't have to remember everything right now. The FBI came in to take over the investigation at Carrington. They rescued several kids. I tracked down Trevor from your contacts and had him come to the hospital to see if he could identify anyone. He knew them all."

It was too much, and his temples were starting to pound. Exhaustion started to pull him under, but he wasn't ready to leave Poe. He wanted to go home.

"I want to go home."

"You will. The doctors just want to make sure they clear whatever Carrington gave you out of your system. Then we'll go home. I missed you in our bed."

He loved the sound of that. Even though he'd given Poe his access code and remote, he hadn't thought his man would want to move in while he was gone.

"You've been staying at my place?"

"Where else would I stay? Now, you get some rest. I want my man to be healthy."

"I'm sorry if you were worried."

"Harmon, I'm going to worry. I care about you, and it comes with the package."

"I do love the package."

"Keep it under your gown until we get home."

He groaned at Poe's playful warning. The confidence that he wasn't back in that clinic drove him to prove his reality was there with Poe. As he fought the oblivion that threatened to drag him back into the darkness, he focused on the touch of Poe's soft hands and even softer lips. Poe seemed to understand that he needed the tether and loved on him until the abyss pulled him back to the uncertainty of sleep.

HIS MAN WAS FINALLY HOME

They hadn't stayed in the hospital long, four days at the most, but he'd thought Harmon needed a few more. Peaches had been by to visit a few times to keep them up to date with what was going on. He didn't care. His man was home. He adjusted the blanket around Harmon and stroked Harmon's forehead. A few weeks had eclipsed, and all his man had done was sleep. Whatever they'd given Harmon had sent the man into a violent bout of withdrawal. The first week had Gibson coming to examine his man at least once a day.

The doctors were positive there wouldn't be any lasting effects from the drugs and shock therapy. But they also couldn't say what the injections were, and it would take a while to work through the research files.

His eyes burned at the thought of the pain Harmon suffered. How could someone hurt another human being the way Carrington had?

The evidence piling up had been enough to sink Carrington if the man had survived. The stories of the men and women inside the facility were nightmare-inducing. Linus had turned over some heavily edited footage of the operation. Some people were omitted like Horace and Freddie since there was some past criminal activity. He'd learned Alex was a former SEAL turned successful businessman. Peaches explained that they didn't want the people who assisted them to be mired down in the legalities.

Charges weren't brought yet, and Peaches was confident it wouldn't come to that. It turned out that Peaches had some friends in murky places. They'd also made a deal they'd turn over all evidence that pertained to the case. Well, whatever they deemed pertinent.

He eased down on the side of the bed and rubbed Harmon's chest. Harmon seemed to calm when he was close, and he had no intention of leaving any time soon. Working from his side of Harmon's bed as the man slept.

"Are you real?" Harmon asked without opening his eyes.

The smallest effort seemed to tire Harmon out, and it worried him. It didn't appear that Harmon was getting any better. Every time Harmon awakened the man asked him was he real.

"Very much so, baby."

"How long have I been asleep?"

The steadier tone of Harmon's voice eased him, but not enough to push away all his worry. The healthy color of his face was back and with the steady meals, Harmon's angles weren't as harsh.

"This time, a few hours."

"I need to piss, and I fucking stink."

His man was so eloquent, but at least his man was becoming more himself.

"You want help or try it yourself?"

"I gotta do it myself."

He had the urge to argue but didn't want to make Harmon feel weak. Harmon had taken care of himself long before he'd come along.

"Want a smoke and then dinner?"

He chuckled at Harmon's almost obscene moan and was jealous he hadn't caused it.

"I'd kill for a smoke and an energy drink."

"Both I can do, Lily keeps coming by. It isn't like you're going to run out anytime soon."

Lily was slowly breaking, and it was almost as bad as remembering the sobs Peaches had let out when she'd seen Harmon the first time after the rescue. Peaches hadn't appeared to be able to touch Harmon enough. Kissed his face and checked every inch of him for wounds. Brushed the slight burns on the man's temples. He didn't blame her. When he'd found out they were putting Harmon through Electroshock when they'd entered the room, he'd felt horrified. Two rounds from what the bastard's recordings had revealed.

Hundreds of tapes were left to go through, and in some ways, Harmon's treatment had been better than others—which disturbed him. Bodies were starting to add up. People not as strong as Harmon who hadn't survived the stages of the so-called treatments.

"Is she okay?"

"Better, but you being asleep every time she comes by is taking its toll on her."

"Call her?"

He leaned over Harmon and used the backs of his fingers to stroke the coarse beard that covered Harmon's cheeks. "Take your shower, and while I get everything ready for you, I'll give her a call. Yell if you need me, don't push yourself too much."

"I promise. Can you make an appointment for me to get groomed?"

"Way ahead of you. If you can stay awake, I'll take you into Powers. Hawthorne is expecting you."

"You're too good to me."

"It will never be good enough."

"Don't feel sorry for me, please."

He stroked his lips across the blunt fringe of Harmon's wet lashes. "Don't cry, baby, I don't feel sorry for you. I'm concerned. I want my crazy Harmon Little back, and I'm here until that happens."

He'd lost count of how many times he wanted to tell Harmon that he loved him again, but since Harmon came home, he'd noticed his man's insecurity grew in intensity. The man seemed to lose himself. Forget where he was and it was worse when he woke up until reality became clearer. That was one of the reasons he'd taken to working from the bed. He was there to reassure Harmon that he wasn't still at the mercy of Carrington and the drugs.

Emotional and mental exhaustion weighed him down, but he didn't obsess over it. He'd pasted a smile on his face no matter how much he didn't feel it just to make sure his man was secure. He hated hiding things from Harmon.

"I thought you were a hallucination when you came to visit. I'm scared you're not real, that meeting you at all wasn't real."

"I'm very much real."

Harmon had tried to initiate sex a few times, but his baby wasn't ready. He'd just upped his affection to soothe his man with plenty of kisses and touches. He'd witnessed too much flinching to push his man too soon.

"Take your shower and don't push too much, you're still healing."

He gave his man one more kiss and let it linger. Then he forced himself away. He made his way to the kitchen and removed a joint from one of the baggies Lily had dropped off. He placed that plus an energy drink and bottle of juice on the broken coffee table. They needed to get some new furniture for the place. He'd even stocked the fridge with real food. He'd sort of taken over since he'd practically moved in.

He flopped down on the couch and picked his phone up from the cluttered surface. He opened his recent calls, and Lily was the last one. He connected the call and waited for the woman to answer.

"Is my son awake?"

It was the same question she asked every time they talked. She didn't care about polite small talk.

"Yes, and he's asking for you."

"Damon and me will be right there."

He didn't even check to see if the call disconnected because he knew she'd hung up on him. He opened his laptop to work on a report and distract himself for a few minutes. He listened to the whine of the pipes when the shower started upstairs. The steady tap of his fingers on the keys hypnotized him, and he lost himself in the repetition of his work.

The squeak of the bedroom door made him jerk his gaze to the metal landing. He pushed himself up and rushed to the stairs. He was halfway up when Harmon held his hand up.

"No, if I fall, I don't want you to get hurt."

He didn't want to obey but didn't want to make Harmon feel weak. His hands painfully clenched around the safety railing on either side of the steps. He inhaled and held it as he counted steps, then he tensed as Harmon seemed to trip but quickly caught himself. Once Harmon was a few steps above him, he reversed until his feet rested on the cement of the floor.

"Lily and Damon are on their way, actually they should be here any minute. I got distracted with work."

"You shouldn't be missing work for me."

"Harmon, I'm not missing anything. Don't even try to start an argument."

"But don't couples make up after they fight?"

A sexy smirk stretched Harmon's gorgeous mouth, and he closed the few steps of distance between them. Harmon was shirtless and his skin slightly damp from his shower and exertion.

"I miss you." Harmon groaned as their mouths met.

"I'm right here."

He tilted his chin and pushed his lips to Harmon's. His tongue sensuously stroked across the full curved of Harmon's mouth.

"But I want you to love on me."

That beautiful whine was so sexy that he couldn't help his body's response to it. His cock tented the cotton of the pajama bottoms he'd borrowed from Harmon. He raised his hands to Harmon's sides and turned him until they were flush. He dug his short nails into Harmon's flesh and savored the deep groan.

"Harmon."

They groaned together at the sound of Lily's voice.

"I need a minute, go spend some time with Lily and I'll be right back."

He didn't wait for Harmon to protest and he jogged up the steps, then he slammed the door shut to lean back on it. He adjusted his hard cock and cursed his lack of control. Harmon didn't have to do more than say his name, and he wanted his man. He strode across the room and pulled open the drawer. Without thinking too much, he removed a condom and a small bottle of lube. He tucked them into his pocket.

Guilt momentary assailed him at the thought of taking his man too soon, but he had other plans. He returned downstairs to the pungent smell of weed. He noticed Damon in the recliner watching Lily on the couch with Harmon's head on her lap.

She stroked Harmon's hair in a motherly way, and he looked so content. He grabbed a chair from beside the kitchen table and set it beside Damon.

Harmon and Lily spoke in hushed tones.

"Thanks for calling, Poe. She hasn't been herself, and I missed my Lily."

Damon's love deepened his voice, and the adoration on the man's face awed him. They'd been married for decades, and the love between the couple was tangible and sweet. He was surrounded by so much happiness, and he'd never really stopped to take it in.

"No need to thank me. I think Harmon needed to see her too. His mother should be here."

"I'll never forget the look on Lily's face the first time she saw Harmon. It was the same expression of love she had for Linus, then with the twins, Lucky and Lou after she'd given birth. Don't get me wrong, she loves all the kids we've adopted as parental figures, but Harmon was different."

"He's an amazing man who doesn't know it."

"That night is when I learned exactly what a gift Lily was to others. To me, she's been my everything, and I truly didn't understand she was that for others too. My heart broke when I saw the joy on his face as Lily hugged him and told him she wasn't ready for him to go home yet."

He took Damon's hand and laced their fingers as they watched mother and son on the couch. In the interaction between the two, he saw his Harmon coming to life. The harshness was softening as the man reveled in Lily's love. She bent forward and brushed her lips to Harmon's forehead, hugging him to her stomach.

"I love you, son."

"I love you too, Mama." Harmon sounded so small.

Tears filled his eyes and spilled down his cheeks. Family had nothing to do with blood, and sometimes the most powerful expressions of familial love were between the people who chose each other. This was what he'd been there for—meant to be a part of Harmon's life. He accepted Damon's hug but didn't stop watching his man soak up Lily's attention.

HOME IS WHERE LOVE EXISTS

*H*armon had a lot of time to think over the past few weeks. The nightmares were still there. That feeling of helplessness was suffocating him and the guilt he didn't feel for killing a man. Carrington wouldn't have stopped because he believed the people he'd experimented on were no more important than data applied to a numbered file.

He was relaxed from his smoke session with Lily and stared up at the steel beams of the ceiling. The darkness had seemed to close in on him, and he'd taken to keeping the spotlights on, but he'd turned them down when Poe had fallen asleep beside him. His man was curled into a ball under a blanket.

Life wasn't the way he had seen it, his past and insecurities had mired him in the bad experiences, made them the largest memories he had. He'd felt shame for so many years, seventeen years of blaming himself for surviving. If his friends could see inside his head, they'd be shocked. Yes, he was crazy and didn't think before he acted, but all of that had hidden his truth.

It had been to keep people away. He'd let the insanity out like a neon sign telling everyone to keep back. That wasn't what happened. He'd found a mother, not just a maternal figure, but a mother who loved him in all his weirdness. A team and family, plus a man all his own.

He knew he probably wouldn't ever get over his past. Too many scars remained, but he had to learn to accept.

"Your thinking woke me up," Poe whined.

He glanced down to study Poe as the man cutely rubbed his eyes, and he gently put Poe's glasses back on so the man could see.

"Sorry."

"Don't be...this is the longest you've been awake since I brought you home. You okay?"

"Yeah, I think"—he paused—"I keep thinking of all the shit I missed out on over the years and took for granted. The first time I tried to kill myself I was thirteen. It was my first night on the streets. I was curled up in a storm drain. My foster family had called to send me back. I couldn't understand why no one wanted to keep me. I lost my virginity a week later for what amounted to one night of a full belly."

"Are those what the marks on your forearm mean?"

Poe lifted his arm to brush his lips against the marks then repeated on the other, and he knew they were still raised and raw after all the time that passed. The numerous scars were reminders not only of survival but his self-loathing. No matter how much ink he'd covered them with, they still existed.

"There's one for each person who used me. I even added a new one after the stalker thing. I hadn't cut myself in so long. You're the first person I've told what they mean."

He relaxed into the cushions as Poe sat up and then shifted to straddle his lap.

"Your secret is safe with me. Do you know what I thought the first time we met?"

"That you were going to die?"

He felt a bit lighter at Poe's husky laugh and slow smile, as if the man were content.

"Well, that too. I couldn't get over how adorable you were."

He groaned and let his head fall onto the back of the couch. "Adorable, cute, they're kisses of death."

Poe pushed against his chest and giggled. "No, not at all. Even though I was frightened about being snatched by some crazy man who had a friend who gave body disposal tips, deep down there was something about you. It's the reason I called you. I'd agonized over it. Said to myself, *Poe, there is no way that man wants you.*"

"Poe." He wanted to stop him. He didn't like when Poe talked bad about himself. To him, the smaller man was just right.

"No, I learned something from you. A lesson that no one else ever got through to me. That I was enough. Just me, just Solomon Poe. In all my geekiness and chubbiness, I was enough. I wanted to do that for you, but then I realized you didn't need me to validate you. Earlier, with you and Lily, I saw the real Harmon Little. A boy who was lost but found his way long before I came along. You just hadn't realized it, Harmon."

He lifted his head until his gaze met Poe's. "I was thinking. I focused so much on the fucking mistakes I made that I never really thought about the fact that my life is pretty good. I got parental units, family, and you. You were the biggest surprise. You wanted to keep me."

"I always want to keep you, Harmon, even if you don't get it."

"Why?"

"Because I love you, Harmon, every crazy, dysfunctional square inch of you. From your gorgeous eyes that don't hide what you're feeling to the tips of your ugly as fuck feet."

He didn't think it was physically possible to have all the oxygen driven from his lungs by three simple words. Words that no more amounted to single syllables but powerful enough to bring men to their knees. He felt embarrassed by it—unworthy of it.

"Ouch, that was so mean. You say you love me, compliment my eyes and then insult me seconds later."

"I love the flaws as well as all the pretty parts. You don't have to say it. I'm not rushing you. I needed you to know, nothing more. No expectations."

He felt like an asshole, but even as the phrase formed perfectly in his mind, his tongue and lips wouldn't conform to the words. Terrified that he hadn't been rescued at all. Poe was the flawless construct of what he wanted his person to be. That he'd always been in that facility and even now still was. Since his rescue, those were the nightmares he suffered through.

"Love on me, please." He'd beg, drop to his knees, and pray to a God he didn't believe in just for a single moment of being loved and loving.

"Baby, you never have to ask."

He almost grabbed Poe to keep him in place but made himself relax his arms to his sides. His hands were fisting in the frayed couch pillows. Poe deserved so much more than the dinginess of his sanctuary. Poe deserved the romance of which he didn't see himself capable.

"Remove your pants, Harmon."

He didn't second-guess the order and placed his feet firmly on the floor as he lifted enough to work his bottoms off. He swallowed hard as Poe began to remove his clothes—bared the creaminess of his soft, velvet skin. The fleshiness of Poe's belly reminded him of how many times he'd rested his head upon it. The spiciness of ginger and vanilla, scents that reminded him of his new home. He let the air from his lungs in a long shuddering breath as his man was finally bare. Poe's cock was hard, and wetness was seeping from the tip.

"Should I turn—"

"No, I want you inside me."

"I love when you fill me."

"I know you do."

His protests ended as Poe bent at the waist, tongue-fucked his mouth gently and Poe's touch sent him to what he thought the mythical Heaven would be like. His cock thickened and he kept his eyes open—he wanted to see Poe's expression. The pleasured flush of his pale cheeks. The familiar click of a cap preceded an ecstasy infused moan as he knew his man prepared himself.

Nervousness tempered his lust as if this were the first time. That no one had done any of this to him before. He loved the gentleness of Poe's lovemaking—it never felt like he was being fucked. Poe's slim fingers fisted in his shaggy hair and then he had a lapful of Poe, then Poe's free hand smoothed lube on his bare cock.

"I've had two clean tests in the last year and haven't been with anyone in almost two."

He stared into Poe's shimmering blue eyes. Recognized the love and need in them.

"I'm clean, I promise." Harmon groaned at the slippery squeeze of Poe's hand, and then the fat head of his dick met Poe's stretched hole.

"You're it for me, do you understand me, Harmon?"

Poe's words stole his voice even as his man slowly lowered onto his cock. His big hands gripped the slight give of Poe's hips but let his man have control of the pace. He encircled Poe in his arms, stroked his palms up the smoothness of his man's back until he curled his hands over Poe's shoulders.

"So fucking perfect." Poe's voice was low and gruff as Poe's ass met his thighs.

The grip of Poe's body almost painful, the strangeness of Poe's heat around his bare dick was almost more than he could take. He'd never realized how much the protection of latex dulled the sensations.

Poe took his mouth in a possessive, hard kiss, biting and sucking on his lips. His man tugged at his lip ring and just as Poe started to move, his man thrust his tongue inside. The slickness of their sweaty bodies moved together in a slow rhythm. The give and take matched in intensity. Moans. Grunts. Sweet whimpers, his and Poe's flowed together in a lustful duet, and his eyes fell shut.

His body tensed in a shudder that worked from his shoulders down to his toes, toes that curled into the plush carpet. Poe pulled his mouth away, and he opened his eyes just to watch. Poe arched and bounced, canted his hips front to back, the sensuous movements flawless as Poe loved on him. He scooted down until he could get enough leverage to thrust up to meet the fall of Poe's body.

He gripped Poe's fuzzy ass cheeks in his hands, felt the jiggle as their bodies met with a gentle slapping of skin. His muscles burned as he took in the beauty of his man from his sweaty hair down to where he watched his shaft disappear into Poe's hole. He needed more.

A dominance he'd rarely felt took over, and he lifted Poe off him. He bent the protesting man over, their knees sinking into the couch. As he thrust back into Poe, a shout tore from his throat. He blanketed his man's back. Sucked at the whorl of Poe's ear.

"Mine, say it." He grunted as he shallowly pounded into Poe's ass.

"Yours, always yours."

"Again," he ordered as he rocked them and the couch with the increased strength and speed of his hips. His breath wheezed from his lungs as he savored every *yours* that passed Poe's lips. He laced his fingers through Poe's where they curved over the back of the couch. He needed that connection.

He caught a high-pitched shriek, and he worked at hitting that spot until Poe whined.

"Fuck!" He pushed through his clenched teeth as the heat took over, burning him up from the inside out and his balls drew up painfully tight.

Poe slammed back onto him and bowed his body. He was lost in the heat and clench, and he ground against Poe's lush ass spilling every drop of cum. Through his own release, he took in the quiver and jerk of Poe's smaller frame. The subtle spasms of his hole milking every last drop of his load.

"Poe," he whispered as he brushed open mouth kisses to his man's sweaty cheek.

"Yes, Harmon."

"I'm going to have you on my dick a lot."

It wasn't romantic, and it wasn't sweet confessions of love, but there wasn't anything better than the happiness of Poe's laughter or the amusement in his man's voice when he finally answered okay.

His decision was sealed, it called for a desperate measure that would be a completely crazy Little move, but he couldn't live without Poe. He was going to make sure Poe knew that the man was the only one for him.

HARMON NEEDED HIM

*H*is body was sore, but he savored the aches and pains from two days of making up for lost time. They'd made love countless times; each time more special than the last. Harmon's promise of having him on his dick a lot hadn't turned into a joke, but he'd felt Harmon come around his cock too. He chuckled to himself as he attempted to work but kept getting distracted.

He'd made up for a lifetime of no sex in mere days. In no way was he complaining. Harmon needed him. Harmon loved him. He knew it despite the fact the man hadn't said it yet. He knew Harmon would say the words when he was ready. Life made Harmon cautious, and he understood and accepted it.

It was a rare moment where he had time to himself to think. Harmon had taken off to get a haircut at Hawthorne and Cress Barbers. Going there was an experience, and as much as he'd wanted to go with Harmon, he wasn't in the mood for the Barbers' crazy antics. They'd become the number one show around Powers since they'd bought the place from the original owner.

He swore those two men would get arrested for one of their

escalating brawls one of these days. Harmon liked the chaos, and he let him have that.

His man was back to normal, well, normal-ish. He still noticed the shadows in Harmon's eyes when the man awakened and needed a few minutes to remember he was home. It wasn't an overnight fix. With everything Harmon had gone through, he'd already made an appointment with Dr. Dahl, the town shrink. Harmon wasn't looking forward to it, but they'd talked and agreed he needed a professional to talk everything through.

Harmon had more to deal with than what happened with Carrington. He knew Harmon was terrified the doctor would find something wrong with him. Harmon complained about what if his brain was broken and he wasn't right.

Harmon was so worried that he would leave. He snorted at the thought. Yes, Harmon tended to be annoying and had a prankster streak a mile wide, but he was harmless. He hadn't thought so when he'd awakened the day before with pink hair and hadn't known it was temporary. Harmon just grinned as he'd jumped around. He wasn't the pink hair type.

He checked the time on his laptop and then closed it deciding on a nap. Weeks' worth of sleep lost, and he was feeling it.

He made his way upstairs and crawled into the messy bed—it smelled like them and sex. He really needed to change the sheets, and he'd do that, later. He reached over the side of the bed and grabbed the blanket, dragging it over him as he pushed his face into Harmon's pillow.

Just the scent of his man relaxed him. The sound of Harmon's gruff voice. His warmth when they cuddled on the couch or in bed. He'd never realized how much the tiny things would be so calming. He yawned as he wiggled deeper into the bed and let sleep take him.

The next thing he remembered was the scruff on Harmon's chin, the warmed metal of his man's lip ring, and he arched into the pleasure of it. He tried to move his arms and realized he was trapped. His eyes flew open, and he stared into mischievous jade eyes.

"What are you doing?" he asked as calmly as he could because he didn't want to be a victim of a Harmon Little special prank. "Why am I tied up?"

"Because you distract me."

Harmon sounded so tranquil as the big man straddled his hips. The man was fully dressed and still wearing his boots. His hair was shaved around the sides and back, longer on top and slightly sticking up. The beard and mustache were gone except for a patch of scruff on his chin and his permanent five o'clock shadow. Harmon looked like his man again. Although he would miss the roughness of Harmon's beard that had left red marks all over his chest and neck, his thighs.

"Harmon, this isn't funny."

"It's not meant to be, and you'll only get out of the cuffs after we have a talk."

"Okay."

"I realized something while I had my free time today."

He didn't answer just waited for Harmon to continue. His man seemed to be trying to concentrate on what he wanted to say.

"Today is the five-month anniversary since I kidnapped you. The best and craziest decision I ever made. I think I loved you the moment I looked into your eyes and straightened your cute glasses."

The only word he had focused on was loved. He wasn't going to ruin the moment by demanding to hear him say it for real. To tell him, *I love you*.

"You looked so shocked, and all I could think was I needed you. Didn't want to leave and not see you again. I know I'm not right and you'll probably get tired of me sooner or later. No, don't deny it, but I ain't letting you go."

"I wouldn't want to go anywhere else."

Harmon answered like he hadn't said a word. "So, I made a decision, you're marrying me, and you're not getting out of the cuffs until you say you will. Lily will do it like she did with everyone else."

His eyes widened until he felt a twinge and stared up at Harmon. Marriage to Harmon, okay, he'd never thought about marriage to anyone. It didn't seem to be in the cards for him, but he wouldn't say the idea didn't cause him joy.

"And why should I marry you?"

Harmon snorted. "Well, you love me, and I love you, Poe. I'm not much of a prize, and you probably got a shitty deal with me, but I'm selfish. Lily and I talked today."

He groaned. Those two talking was never good.

"I'm too old to be adopted, but Little doesn't mean all that much. Lily and Damon want me to be a Trenton, so, you'd have to be Solomon Trenton. It's just the way it's gonna be."

Harmon crossed his arms and pouted, but he couldn't help but be amused by the fact the huge man was acting like a two-year-old.

Lily and Damon wanted Harmon to be a part of the family.

"How do you feel about being a Trenton?"

"It's nothing but a name—"

"Harmon, how do you feel about it?"

"They want me, Poe. Me, all fucked-up and everything, they want—" Harmon's voice broke.

He tugged at the cuffs, but it was a no go. "Come down here."

Harmon lowered himself until their mouths almost touched.

"No matter if your last name is Little or Trenton, you were always theirs. And I would be honored to be Solomon Trenton and belong to your crazy as fuck family."

Harmon's lips slamming down on his took him by surprise, and Harmon's hot breath fanned across his cheek from where Harmon's breath moved heavily in and out through his nose.

"We haven't fucked with one of us in handcuffs yet." Harmon smiled against his mouth.

"That is true...I'm always up for a new experience."

He didn't recognize his voice as he spoke, his shirt split down the middle as he felt the cool, blunt side of a blade stroke up his stomach and chest. His pants were the next to go. Harmon eased off the bed and stripped, and then his man was flush against his side. His man's rough hands were so gentle as they caressed every inch of him.

"I love you, Poe." Harmon shyly whispered the words and looked up at him from under his lashes.

Only time would rid Harmon of his insecurity. Time and love, and he had plenty of both to give Harmon.

"I love you too, Harmon."

"I'm so glad I kidnapped you."

His laugh ended on a moan as his man started to love on him. No rush or race to the finish. Even when it was out of control—visceral—they still savored every touch and sensation. The perfection was in the minute details. The barest of touches. He knew his man could be content with nothing more than kissing. And it would always be about what made his man satisfied. They were more than some one-night stand or fleeting moments of afterglow.

It was caring, anyone could whisper empty words of love, but to care and cherish, that's when it was true. Actions spoke so much louder than words ever could.

EPILOGUE

DEVIL DUST!

A month of wedded bliss, and this was the life. *Harmon Trenton.* He played the name over in his head so many times he'd lost count. He watched the sparkling display of lights on the ceiling and caught his morning buzz as Poe slept peacefully beside him.

He turned his head to the side and couldn't get over how cute his husband was—husband, still a bit of a weird concept. He returned his attention to the ceiling. He'd held onto his hope that Poe wouldn't run before they exchanged vows. First, they'd gone through the name change with Peaches making sure it went quickly. The judge had signed it while he'd stood there, Lily and Damon on either side of him. Lucky, Lou, and Linus on the bench behind him. Poe was under Damon's arm.

It was perfect. He still looked at his new ID every day to make sure it hadn't changed.

Then later that afternoon, Poe had said *I do* in the backyard of Lily's house. He cherished every milestone. Made sure to keep track of anniversaries, even the small silly ones no one else would care about. Poe deserved to know how much he was appreciated and that he'd never take the smaller man for granted.

Poe was his gift, his reward for surviving.

He placed the roach in the ashtray on the nightstand and turned to his side. He brought his hand to Poe's glitter-covered chest. Yellow, his favorite color. The tiny sparkling specks coated his fingertips as he stroked them down Poe's body.

Poe hummed, and his eyelids slowly fluttered open. As always, his husband greeted him with a smile.

"What time did you get home?"

"About an hour ago."

"Old man Simpson still getting it on with Mrs. Harrison or what's his new flavor of the week?"

"I don't know how he keeps up with them. He barely gets around on that cane of his. They must have given him bionic hips his last replacement."

Poe tilted his head to the side as if studying him. "Harmon, why are you sparkly? You getting lap dances on the clock?"

He would've felt the need to defend himself, but Poe's smile was amused and bright.

"I like shiny things."

"Why am I itching?" Poe asked as he rubbed his chest.

He froze as he watched Poe look down at where the man was scratching.

"Harmon Trenton, what the hell did you do?"

Poe was out of the bed and standing there with his hands on his naked hips, covered in yellow glitter.

"I was watching the sparkles reflect on the ceiling, disco ball style!"

He sat up naked in bed and crossed his legs.

"How much did you smoke?" Poe demanded and then rushed off toward the bathroom.

"I got bored waiting for you to wake up," he protested and swung his legs over the side of the bed and followed his husband's rounded ass with his gaze.

"Harmon, what is the rule?"

"Don't mess with Poe while he's sleeping."

"Exactly."

"But, Poe, I got bored." He stretched bored out until Poe glared at him.

"Look at me, Harmon."

"Sexy and sparkly," he whispered huskily and approached his husband as the man backed up into the huge shower stall.

"No, Harmon, we're not having sex while I'm covered in glitter."

"But…but…Poe, you're so shiny, and it's my favorite color." He pouted because he knew Poe couldn't resist him. "You know I gotta have you on my dick, it's how it works. I mess up, and we do the whole makeup sex thingie. It's amazing." He batted his lashes, and mentally fist-pumped at the small twitch of Poe's lips.

"Harmon, we are not—"

"But, Poe, ya know ya wanna." He crowded Poe back against the shower wall.

"You covered me in Devil Dust," Poe yelled.

"But, Poe, you know the rules, it's how it works."

"But, Harmon, you wash me first."

"Yes," he shouted and turned on the shower.

He might not be right in the head. He wasn't perfect, but Poe loved him anyway. Even when he covered Poe in Devil Dust, his man loved him because he belonged to Poe.

"Why do I love you again, Harmon?" Poe asked with a groan.

"Because you're mine."

THE END

ABOUT THE AUTHOR

J.M. Dabney is a multi-genre author who writes mainly LGBT romance and fiction. She lives with a constant diverse cast of characters in her head. No matter their size, shape, race, etc. she lives for one purpose alone, and that's to make sure she does them justice and give them the happily ever after they deserve. J.M. is dysfunction at its finest and she makes sure her characters are a beautiful kaleidoscope of crazy. There is nothing more she wants from telling her stories than to show that no matter the package the characters come in or the damage their pasts have done, that love is love. That normal is never normal and some-times the so-called broken can still be amazing.

CPSIA information can be obtained
at www.ICGtesting.com
Printed in the USA
FSHW02n0835240618
49762FS